"That will be the day when I let that fat creep adopt me and give me his name. Can you imagine —Chloris Mancha?" She made a wry face. "It makes me sound like *him*."

"You wouldn't have wanted any of the others for your last name, either," Jenny pointed out. "Lunn, Hart, Sherry, Swanson, or Shepherd."

Chloe narrowed her eyes. "Right on. My name is Chloris Carpenter. My real name. Yours is Jenny Carpenter." Her hazel eyes became slits. "You got that? Jenny *Carpenter!*"

KIN PLATT, formerly a well-known cartoonist, is the author of the much admired books *Hey, Dummy* and *The Boy Who Could Make Himself Disappear,* as well as the highly successful mystery stories *Sinbad and Me* and *Mystery of the Witch Who Wouldn't,* all available in Laurel-Leaf editions. Mr. Platt lives in Los Angeles.

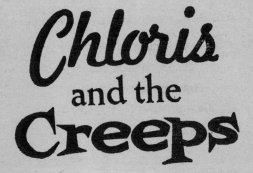

Chloris
and the
Creeps

KIN PLATT

To John F. Marion

Published by
DELL PUBLISHING CO., INC.
1 Dag Hammarskjold Plaza
New York, New York 10017

ISBN: 0-440-91415-9

RL: 5.4

Reprinted by arrangement with Chilton Book Company
Printed in the United States of America
First Laurel printing—September 1974
Ninth Laurel printing—October 1981

CHAPTER 1

IT WAS a gray soggy day in January. The kind we have sometimes in sunny Southern California. My sister Chloris and I were in my room waiting for Mom to come home from her job to fix us dinner. We were sitting on the rug trying to put together a new jigsaw puzzle which, according to the box cover, was supposed to end up looking like a barnyard. It had about a million pieces and none of them matched. Chloris was doing most of the work.

I had never seen a real barnyard in my whole life. Cows, chickens, ducks, geese. Horses. A barn. Little runty pigs and a big fat mama pig. My sister Chloris had never seen a barnyard either. It didn't stop her from trying to put one together. She picked up a yellow jagged piece that looked like part of a duck and set it down next to a crooked brown and white piece that looked like the side of a cow.

"What do you think of Mom's new boy friend?" she asked suddenly.

I thought for a second and shrugged. "He's okay, I guess."

Chloris frowned, tossed her head and slammed her hand down on the rug, making several pieces jump out of place. "He's not okay," she said angrily. "He's a creep."

"How do you figure that?"

She pushed back her long brown hair and scowled. "You don't have to figure it. A creep is a creep."

"Yes, but . . ."

Chloris stopped me by waving her hands. "I'll tell you one thing. If Mom marries that creep I'll never speak to him as long as I live."

I was eight and Chloris was eleven, so she had a long way to go if she meant to keep her promise. "Why? What's Mr. Lunn ever done to us?"

"That's not the point," Chloris said loftily. "The point is, I'm not going to speak to that creep ever. If they decide to get married, just you watch." She bent low over the puzzle. "How did this stupid duck's head get on that dumb cow anyway?" she suddenly yelled, throwing the piece aside and trying unsuccessfully to slide in another one about the same size. "This sure is a stupid puzzle," she said. She straightened up and punched me high on my arm. "Are you?"

"Am I what?"

"Going to speak to that creep?"

"I don't know. Maybe." I rubbed my arm where her fist landed. Chloris is only about three years older than I but, though I hate to admit it, she's a much harder puncher. "That one hurt," I told her.

"That's what I mean about what a creep he is," Chloris said. "Even discussing him like this in a friendly way can be painful."

"You're not supposed to hit in a discussion." I wasn't sure that was a rule but it seemed reasonable. "Anyway, Mom has to get married some time, doesn't she? She's still young."

"So what?" Chloris found another piece to fit. "How about that?" she crowed. "I'll lick this dumb thing yet. How long have we been on it—two hours?"

"Two and a half," I said. Chloris hates fractions or little pieces of anything. She likes everything all together, in one piece. But my arm still hurt and I gave her the fraction. "Besides, Mom keeps telling us we need a father. So maybe that's why she picked Mr. Lunn—to be our father."

Chloris pounded the rug with her fist again and a few more puzzle pieces lost their places, but it was a lot easier on my arm. "We don't need a father. We already had a father."

"Well, what good is that? He's dead."

"Now you did it," she yelled. "You broke the rule." She reached down for the puzzle and savagely yanked the fitted pieces apart, scattering them across the room.

"What are you doing that for?" I asked. "And, what rule?"

"Never talk about the dead," Chloris said, so mad she was almost crying. "*That* rule."

"I never heard of it. I'm sorry, Chloe."

"It's too late to be sorry. You said it. You brought the subject up."

"So what?"

"Don't you see? It's people like you who forget things that are important. And then the next thing you know they don't even mind forgetting all about him and getting a new father."

"Well, maybe," I said. "Anyway I said I was sorry."

"A lot of good that does now," Chloris was still shouting. "Maybe you want to be a Lunn. Not me."

"I really don't care," I said. "We're not Carpenters, either. It's only a name."

"Robert Lunn," Chloris said sarcastically. "Some name!"

It didn't sound that bad to me. But when my sister gets wound up she explodes in all directions. It's her nature.

I picked at a thread in the carpet. "To tell you the truth, Chloe, I honestly hardly even remember him—Daddy, I mean."

She looked down at me. "Now that's a dumb thing to say. How can you not remember your own father?"

"Well, I don't. Not really. I was only two years old when they got divorced, and I only saw him a little after that on the visits."

"You ought to remember him. He was nice."

"Are you sure?"

"Of course, I'm sure," she said angrily. "Real nice."

"Then how come Mom was always crying and they finally got divorced."

Chloris shrugged. "She didn't understand him, probably. Anyway, women are always crying. You see it all the time on TV."

"Not all the time," I said. "Mostly they're talking about how white their washing is."

"Oh, those are only the dumb commercials, dumbbell," Chloris said. "I'm talking about the real-life movies. You watch and see. They're always crying."

"Why?"

"How should I know? Maybe they just like to."

"Maybe," I said. "But anyway Daddy died when I was only five. Wasn't it about three years ago."

Chloris' face was very pale. "You know very well when he died," she said and walked out of the room. Her door slammed, telling me she was mad and wanted to be alone.

It wasn't the first time I had made Chloris walk out on me upset and angry, and as usual I wished I hadn't said what I had. It was too late now to explain or apologize. You couldn't take anything back with her. Whatever you had said remained in the air, growing bigger than you ever imagined. The only thing left to do was wait, hoping this invisible shadowy wall between us would dissolve. It took time.

I looked out the window. The sky was as cheerless as I, sodden with rain. I tossed the scattered jigsaw puzzle pieces into the box with the cover that said: YOUR OWN BARNYARD PUZZLE. PUT THE PIECES TOGETHER AND HAVE HOURS OF SATISFYING FUN. A DELIGHTFUL CHALLENGE FOR MYSTERY LOVERS OF ALL AGES.

I stared at the jumbled cut-outs in the box. You would never imagine that when put together that clutter would look exactly like the picture on the cover. I suddenly realized that I had never before considered a jigsaw puzzle a mystery. It had always been just a game fitting the odd-shaped pieces together until they made sense.

My life was like that. Pieces I remembered that fit, then a lot of missing pieces that left gaping holes. Perhaps Chloris was right in walking away angrily when I said I couldn't remember our father. All I had were little pieces of him, pieces to a puzzle that didn't fit.

"It's your own private jigsaw puzzle," I told myself. "All you have to do is find the missing pieces and put them together. Then it will become a complete picture like the barnyard on the cover and make some sense."

The rain swept down my window. Outside the giant palms bent, lashed by the gale. It was easier to remember him in the rain. Rain and water.

He had a big boat. Saturdays Chloris and I used to visit him there. The harbor was a quiet little inlet off the Pacific Ocean called Marina del Naviero. Sometimes it was swept by a storm and then it was not so quiet, the air and surf roaring in my ears, the big boat tossing and rolling with the swelling waves. We didn't leave the harbor on those days but stayed put, lashed to the pier of the marina, and sang to forget we were frightened.

Then, suddenly, there wasn't going to be any more singing on his boat. No more crying on the way home. Mom was telling us about the new situation. Her face didn't give us a hint.

"Sit down, girls." She patted the sofa. "Sit next to me here, Jenny."

Chloris was looking at me as if to ask had I done anything? I shook my head. We plopped down on opposite sides of Mom, and waited while she studied her hands folded on her lap. She cleared her throat and began. It didn't take long.

"Your father is dead, girls," she said.

That was three years ago, when I was five. They had become divorced three years before that. I couldn't remember much. I was a baby. What do you know when you're only two?

After Mom divorced him Daddy got married again. She got a job at Bontel's Department Store, in the Beauty Salon section selling cosmetics.

I remember Daddy had a new little baby with his new wife. His name was Jeff. Then something happened and he left them. I didn't know why. I didn't understand any of it. I didn't understand why he was suddenly dead.

Right after the divorce, before the second marriage, Daddy used to see Chloris and me on his visiting days—Wednesday nights and Saturdays.

Sometimes he was late, or would call explaining he couldn't make the Wednesday nights because of business. Or sometimes he had to cancel because he wasn't feeling too well, he said. Mom would get very angry, because we would be all dressed up waiting to go out and have dinner with him. She would shout and argue over the phone.

"You can't do that to the girls," she said, going on about how he was disappointing us.

It's one of the sad things that I don't remember feeling disappointed.

After Daddy missed too many Wednesdays night dinner dates with us, the visits came usually on Saturdays. He would ring the bell about ten o'clock in the morning and wait outside. Sometimes Mom had us outside first, waiting for him, but he wasn't always on time and she would get pretty annoyed. He never came into the house except once when he said he had an important phone call to make. Mom didn't say anything, just made a gesture with her hand to where the phone was in the living room, and walked into the kitchen. I heard tap water running and dishes being moved around. Daddy seemed to be talking to some girl, his voice very low, and he kept explaining about how sorry he was that he was going to be late. After he hung up and mopped his face with his handkerchief, he called into the kitchen to thank Mom for letting him use the phone. She didn't answer and he shrugged, smiled mysteriously at Chloris and me, and we went out.

He had a big black convertible Caddy and he

would drive very fast with the windows down. It was cold sometimes, even in Southern California. When I complained about the wind hurting my ears he would look at me and frown. Chloris made believe she didn't mind the wind and would jab me with her elbow and give me a dirty look for spoiling the fun. Most of the time she was the one who came down with the sore throat or infected ear.

We would go to a drive-in for a quick lunch: Hamburgers with Coke. Tacos. He could eat three of them. After that, he would take us out to the marina to his boat.

When Mom told us he was dead she didn't go into any big act pretending she was heartbroken. She just told us straight out, almost without expression. I remember looking from her face to Chloris' who still hadn't said anything. Her head was cocked a little to the side and she was studying her shoes as if she had never seen them before. She made her toes curl up a little, and then straightened them.

Mom cleared her throat again. I noticed how much paler she was. "You might as well know the truth now, girls. It wasn't any accident. Your father shot himself."

I should have asked why, I guess, but I think maybe I was too embarrassed. Chloris didn't say a word, either. She just kept looking down at her old shoes which she was wiggling now from side to side. Finally she spoke.

"Can we go now?"

Mom looked at her, a strange expression in her eyes. As if she were measuring Chloris for the first time.

"Yes, of course," she said abruptly.

Chloris went to her room and closed her door. I went to mine.

I wonder why he did that.

CHAPTER 2

IT WAS a Friday evening after dinner. The door-
bell rang, and there was this stranger with a red
beard. Mom got up, smoothed her skirt, asked
him in and introduced us.

"Mr. Lunn is a business associate," Mom said.
"I've told him about you girls. This seemed like a
good time for us all to know each other better."

Mr. Lunn smiled and leaned down toward me.
"What's your real name—is it Jane or Jennifer?"

"Jenny. Jenny Carpenter."

He nodded and straightened up, still smiling.
"Jenny is a nice name."

"What's yours?" I asked.

"Robert. You can call me Bob, if you like."

I glanced nervously at Mom. "She said Mr.
Lunn."

"My friends call me Bob."

I didn't know what to say then. I looked back at
Chloris standing behind me unsmiling, kind of
bored and tired. Mr. Lunn leaned down again and
started giving Chloris the same treatment.

"What's your name?" he asked.

"Carpenter," Chloris said.

"I know," he said patiently. "Your first name."

Chloris stood there with set lips and I knew she wasn't going to talk.

"It's Chloris," I said quickly. "Chloe, for short."

Mr. Lunn smiled at me. "Thank you. I never would have guessed it." He turned his eyes to my sister. "That's an unusual name, isn't it. Chloris, I mean."

She looked right into his eyes and shrugged.

"You're being spoken to, Chloris," Mom said.

Chloris blinked. "Uh-huh," she said to Mr. Lunn.

He nodded and rocked back on his heels.

"All right, girls," Mom said. "Say goodnight and go back to your rooms and play."

I said goodnight and Mr. Lunn said goodnight. Chloris made believe she was saying it but really what she mumbled could have been anything. I followed her into her room. She closed the door and leaned against it.

"I hate him," she said.

"Gy," I said. "What for?"

"You know what for. He's a creep."

We watched TV for a while without talking. Then Chloris said angrily, "You shouldn't have told him my name."

"Why not?" I said. "He probably heard it anyway from Mom."

"Then why did he ask me?"

"I don't know. Maybe to be friendly."

Chloris tossed her long hair. "He's wasting his time. I hate him. I hate her for bringing him here."

"What for?" I said puzzled. I was about to say something else and changed the words just in time. "She's not married."

"That's no excuse," Chloris said. "A person is supposed to wait a decent time before they get married again."

"More than six years?"

Looking at me Chloris' eyes were hard. "You know something? You've got the makings of a first-class creep."

I didn't mind her calling everybody else that. But I knew I wasn't any creep.

"Daddy got married again," I reminded her. "He married that girl who used to be his secretary. Remember?"

Chloris lay back on her bed, her eyes closed. "Turn up the TV when you get a chance. I can still hear you."

"He got married again right after the divorce. I don't think he even waited a year. Her name was Cindy. Don't you remember?"

"You remember for me. I got enough problems."

"When he used to take us down to his office on Saturdays, she was the one he asked to talk to us while he did his work. Remember?"

"You got it all wrong, dumbbell," Chloris said. "It wasn't Cindy. It was Jackie."

"No, it wasn't. Jackie was the one who was such

a good swimmer. The one who always laughed a lot."

Chloris frowned. "Maybe. I never liked her much anyway."

After the divorce he got the boat. After stepping over the side, you walked down a few steps into what was like a very small apartment. It had a tiny kitchen called a galley. The bed, a narrow cot built into the wall, was called a bunk. There were two of them. There were narrow closets for dishes and pots. The bathroom had two names. John and head. Daddy said he lived on the boat. He had electric light and running water. Boats in the marina were tied up close to each other, and he had a lot of neighbors.

Sometimes he took us out to sea for a ride. The engine was very noisy and we bounced a lot, but it was fun even though we were almost always cold and wet. On the days we didn't go out on the water he had us clean and polish. We each got a quarter if we did the job right.

He had a girl friend then called Sandra. I don't remember much about her because I was busy cleaning and polishing while they were talking. Later we would go out for something to eat. Sometimes we went over to his girl friend's house. She made sandwiches for us, and gave us Cokes and milk.

At first, after we came home Mom would ask us what kind of a day did we have. Both Chloris and I were too embarrassed to talk much about Sandra. Mom caught on and cut her questions short. Like, did we have a good time? We told her yes, we did, and that was all.

A few months later Daddy had a new girl friend. "What happened to Sandra?" I asked him.

"Little girls like you wouldn't understand," he said. "Forget it."

The one after that one was Lila, not too different from Sandra except that she wasn't too happy when he dragged us along. She never had any milk at her place and she made terrible sandwiches. But she always had some candy for us.

I liked Jackie. She was tall and blonde and a terrific swimmer. She laughed a lot, even when Chloris and I stopped working to watch them. She had big white teeth.

Then it was the girl at his office. Cindy. Mom wasn't too happy the day Chloris and I told her we had just been over to Daddy's new wife's apartment.

"New wife?" she said. "Are you sure?"

"That's what he said," Chloris said. "His new wife. Why? Is there some kind of law against it?"

Mom looked at Chloris, her face white and drawn. "No. No law at all. He's entitled to start a new life and get married again if he wishes." She got up to turn something off on the kitchen range. "Just like I am," she added, and went into her room.

The next thing I heard was that he left Cindy even before his new baby was born. He was supposed to have found a new girl. Then he shot himself and it was all over. I don't remember much about it and maybe Chloris is right—I am a dumbbell with a rotten memory. He didn't leave any of those suicide notes you read about to explain anything. He didn't send us a letter telling how much he loved us and how we should grow up good and healthy and strong and to always love our mother. Nothing.

We didn't even get to go to the funeral. He wasn't Mom's husband any more, for one thing. And I imagine she didn't have any deep feelings about him since he left her for another woman. I could understand that. Not at the time it happened, of course. Later. At the time it happened I couldn't understand anything.

When Mr. Lunn came along, I wondered if Mom would really marry him. He seemed okay but would it be right for us to love Mr. Lunn if and when he became our new father? I wanted to discuss it with Chloris but she didn't want to talk about it. Once she made it perfectly clear why.

"I don't even want to think about it," she said grimly. "We already had a father."

What good was that? I wanted to say. He was dead, and I could hardly remember him.

The trouble was I wasn't sure we really needed a new father. After all, we had Mom. She took care of us fine, and she wasn't a stranger.

CHAPTER 3

"WHAT if I run away?" Chloris asked. "Can you take care of yourself?"

I shrugged. "Anyway, why do you want to run away?"

"To teach her a lesson not to marry that old creepy Bob Lunn."

We were in her room. It's kind of wild. A lot of things hang down from the ceiling that spin and turn, called mobiles. Chloris made them out of paper and cardboard, stapled them together, attached black thread and hung them from nails in the ceiling. There are an awful lot of them. When you lie down on her bed, face up, it's like being in a jungle. She made a few for my room but frankly I'm not too crazy about them. They're always moving and make me nervous.

Her walls were covered with posters and pictures, bought with her weekly allowance money. I don't think there was a square inch of wall showing. One of them said PEACE. Another said LOVE. One I liked said HELP STAMP OUT POTATO CHIPS. Chloris loved potato chips.

It was the first time she had ever mentioned the idea of running away.

"You're kidding," I said. "What would you do without all this?" I waved my hand at all the decorations in her room.

"Big deal," Chloris said. "I can always get more."

"Where would you get the money?"

"I'll get a job."

"You're not old enough to get a job," I said. "Besides, how will you be able to do your homework?"

"I hadn't thought about that. Maybe I'll go to school in Cleveland."

Cleveland was where Daddy's mother lived. Grandma Helen. Short and pudgy, with short blonde hair, very peppy and able to talk a blue streak. Once in a while she sent us each five dollars. It came on a check. Along with the check was a short note that said *Remember your father!*

I think Grandma Helen was the one responsible for Chloris being on such a downer after Daddy died. She came to California for the funeral and to see us afterwards with Grandpa Bert. They took us out to dinner. Mom didn't come. She wasn't too crazy about Grandma Helen.

Grandma Helen kept talking into Chloris' ear all through the meal. I couldn't help hearing a lot of it because her voice carried.

"Your father was a great man," she said. "A very brilliant man. If you ask me, your mother never appreciated him. I'm not saying that as criticism, mind you. But I don't think she ever really tried to make my son happy."

Chloris looked down at her half-eaten hamburger and pushed it away. "I guess so," she said tonelessly.

"I brought my son up to appreciate the joy of life," Grandma said. "Now he's dead at only thirty-seven. You wouldn't say he had much chance to appreciate life to die so young, would you?"

Chloris pushed out her lower lip. "I guess not."

"Grandma," I said. "Daddy wasn't married to Mom any more when he died. He was married to Cindy."

She sat back and looked down at me. Her lips twisted and her eyes weren't too friendly. "You may be too young to be able to discuss this intelligently, Jennifer. But the way I feel about it is, if your mother had tried to make Larry happy he wouldn't have got divorced. And then maybe he wouldn't have done this terrible foolish thing."

Later, after they had brought us home and left, I said to Chloris, "She made it sound as if Mom did it. Like it was her fault he committed suicide."

Chloris looked angrily at me. "Well, what about it? They were husband and wife, weren't they?"

"What's that got to do with it?" I thought about two girls I knew at school whose parents got divorced. "Cheryl Lee's mother got remarried and so did her father. He didn't do anything to himself. The same with Alice Farmer. Her mother divorced *her* father. He didn't get married again yet but he didn't do anything desperate. He still comes around to visit and take her out."

"So what? Nobody ever said they all do. Maybe Daddy had a worse home life than those others."

Now I looked Chloris right in the eye. "You mean you'd go to live with Grandma Helen in Cleveland?"

"Maybe. She said I had a standing invitation."

"What does that mean—standing invitation?"

"It means I'm invited there any time I want to go."

"Mom wouldn't let you," I said. "I don't think she likes Grandma Helen too much."

That was probably all my fault. When we got home that night after dinner with Grandma Helen and Grandpa Bert Mom asked me how we spent the evening. I told her, then asked if it were true that Daddy didn't have a happy home life with her. She stared.

"What makes you ask that?"

"Something Grandma said—to Chloris."

She asked what it was and I told her, her eyes opening so wide I thought they would pop. "Of all the things to say to a child," Mom finally said when she got her breath. "Of all the vicious things to say!"

When I asked her what she meant, she only shrugged and refused to answer, then sat staring out the window twisting her hands, very pale.

"I'm sorry," I told her that night. "I didn't think it was true. I don't think even Chloris believed her. She just kept on and on about it. I

told her Daddy wasn't even married to you when
... when. ..."

Mom stood up, smoothing her skirt. "I'll tell you
one thing," she said, her voice shaking. "I'm never
having that woman step foot in my house again.
Never!"

She stormed out of the living room and banged
on Chloris' door.

"What is it?" Chloris asked from inside.

Mom threw the door open. "I understand your
grandmother had been filling your head with a lot
of vicious lies. I just told your sister she is not
welcome in this house any longer. If you want to
write her, or visit with her when she comes, you
will meet her outside."

Chloris didn't look up. "Okay," she muttered.
"Okay."

"Another thing. It takes a special kind of person
to say what she did to my daughters out of my
sight. It takes the same kind of person to bring
up a son who would do what he did, what your
father did. Do you understand what I'm saying?"

Chloris shrugged, keeping her face down.

"Answer me!" Mom demanded. I couldn't remember her ever being so angry. "Look at me."

Chloris finally lifted her head. "I guess," she
said.

"You guess," Mom repeated. She looked wildly
around the room. Then she leaned down toward
Chloris. "Do you really believe that? That I made
your father's home life so unhappy that he . . .
that he killed himself?"

"I don't know. I don't remember much about it. I was too young."

Mom blinked. "Yes," she said finally. "I suppose you were."

Mom walked out stiffly and that was the last word she ever said on the subject. Chloris told me I was a creep for blabbing what Grandma said, and I told her I didn't care. It wasn't the first time we ever had a fight.

Now we were back on the same subject. Grandma Helen. I couldn't believe Chloris would leave me and Mom to live with her.

"Maybe Mom won't marry Mr. Lunn after all," I said. "Then your troubles will be over."

"I'm not so sure," Chloris said. "If she doesn't marry him, it's only going to be someone else. She's got it into her head to get married again. I know it."

"So what? Maybe it's a good idea. She works too hard."

Chloris laughed. "Are you kidding? Whatever gave you that idea?"

"Well, she comes home tired, doesn't she?"

Chloris waved her arms. "That's the traffic she has to drive through. Not the job. Bontel's is a very swanky store. They wouldn't ask anybody who works for them to work too hard."

"Maybe it's harder selling cosmetics, like she does. Maybe a lot of women don't want to buy the stuff and she has to work hard to convince them."

Chloris put a record on her small player machine. It was one of the early Beatles I liked. *Hey*

Jude. She threw herself down on her bed.

"You're like my record player," she said. "You just go around and around."

"Maybe," I said. "What if you ever got married and then had to get divorced? Wouldn't you ever get married again with another husband?"

"Not me. I won't have that problem because I don't intend to ever get married."

I was shocked. "You mean you're going to be a virgin?"

"I guess so. If you want to know the truth, I'm not too crazy about men."

"I like Mr. Lunn's red beard," I said. "If he ever marries Mom I'd like to see how he shaves it."

Chloris got up and shut her record player off. *Hey, Jude* came to a stop right in the middle of a sentence. "You've got a terrible one-track mind, Jen. I already told you I don't want him for a father."

"I don't know why you're pretending you were so crazy about Daddy," I said angrily. "He was always hitting you and making you cry."

Chloris glared at me. "That's not true. He never hit me."

"Yes, it is. He hit you when you didn't run to him and kiss him when he came home. I remember."

Chloris sniffed. "Well, maybe once. Anyway, I suppose I had it coming. I probably hurt his feelings."

"He hit you later when you didn't bring a good

report card to show him." Suddenly I remembered that, too.

"Big deal. All fathers do that."

"He hit you when you weren't nice to Cindy," I said.

Chloris got very pale. Little beads of sweat sparkled on her forehead. She grabbed for my arms and started to shake me. "It's not true," she cried. "Take it back. It's not true."

"Yes, it is," I said, trying to break away, but she was too strong. "He hit you when you didn't want to eat the sandwich she made you and when you said you wanted to go home to Mom."

Suddenly Chloris released my arms, jumped off the bed, ran to her door and threw it open.

"Get out!" she screamed. "You're making it all up. He never hit me. He always loved me. He said I was his favorite girl. He said he was going to marry me some day."

I stared. "How could he do that?"

She picked up a small pillow and threw it at me. She missed and I went out. She slammed the door behind me. I hadn't taken two steps away when I heard her crying. It was the hardest crying I ever heard Chloris do.

CHAPTER 4

AFTER school I went to visit a school friend, Beverly Brandon, exactly my age. Beverly has an older sister and two brothers. Her mother is divorced, like we are, and she doesn't have another father for her children, either. She doesn't exactly work. She goes to college studying to be some kind of a doctor.

Because she is very friendly, when I had a chance I asked her, "What kind of a doctor, Mrs. Brandon?"

"Speech pathologist," she said. "There are a lot of children and grown-ups who can't speak properly."

"Is it expensive?" I asked. "I mean, going back to college again to be a doctor."

"Yes. But George helps me. He's a lawyer and quite successful. It's only fair. When he was going to college I worked and helped put him through even though I was on that high school-college-childbirth track. I married young, so I didn't realize I, too, had the choice of another life style."

My friend Beverly was pretty relaxed and didn't

mind my talking to her mother. "Is it okay if I ask your mother a kind of personal question?"

"Why not?"

"It's not really personal," I said. "I guess it's just a question."

Beverly shrugged. "Ask her anyway."

Mrs. Brandon had dashed into the kitchen to put something in the oven. That gave me enough time to think of how to ask, and when she came back I was almost ready.

"Did I hear you say you wanted to ask me a question, Jenny?"

I liked the direct way she spoke to me. No phony politeness.

"Are you going to get another father for your children?"

She didn't even have to think about it. She smiled and pushed back her hair. "Why? Do you think they need another father?"

I had to answer, because after all, it was my own dumb question. "I don't know. I guess it's because my Mom got divorced, too. And lately she's been talking a lot about it."

"Well," Mrs. Brandon said, "I'd say that was up to her. You see, here we don't go into that bag about having another husband, or another father. I just go out on dates."

My mouth opened. "Dates?"

She nodded. "Dates. I go out about four times a week."

I looked over at Beverly calmly reading her book.

"I don't think my sister Chloris would like that," I said. "I mean, if our Mom went out on dates. A lot, I mean."

Mrs. Brandon smiled again. "My children and I have no problem about it. They accept my dating as part of my being an adult entitled to a life of my own. My children have their social life and I have mine."

"Gy," I said. "But . . . but . . . are these different dates—I mean, different men you date?"

"It all depends," she said, shrugging her shoulders. "There's no special one, if that's what you mean. Because of your similar situation you're probably wondering how my children react. I don't involve them. I don't want people wandering in and out of their lives."

I wanted to get it straight. "What does that mean?"

"It means simply that I am trying to become my own person. My children don't have to go up or down with my affairs. I keep them tending to their own affairs. When they need me, I'll be around and available." She patted my head gently. "Loving somebody doesn't mean you have to hang over them every minute, you know."

There wasn't much for me to say after that except my goodbyes. Beverly only lived a few blocks from me but walking home gave me time enough to go over everything Mrs. Brandon had said.

Chloris was off with some of her own friends so I got going on my homework, especially some problems in new math that were really a pain.

She came in about an hour later and went straight to her room. I could tell she was in one of her don't-talk-to-me-I-want-to-be-alone moods. I heard her radio going. Then she cut it off and turned on her TV. Then she turned off her TV and put on some records. She was upset about something. About three records later, she knocked on my door.

"Don't disturb me," I said. "I'm working."

"On what?" she asked, coming in.

I showed her my math book and she made a face. "Where were you?" she asked.

"Beverly Brandon invited me over her house."

"Beverly Brandon? Doesn't she have a brother?"

She knew as well as I did that Beverly had a brother. He was tall and good-looking and in Chloris' class. That was the one she meant. Beverly had another brother, too. But he was much younger than Mark, the one Chloris liked, and I knew she wasn't counting him. His name was Nicky and he was even too young for me.

"Mark wasn't home," I said. "Mrs. Brandon was."

After Mom came home and fixed us dinner I had a chance to talk to her while Chloris was in her room studying. I told her about Mrs. Brandon, getting most of it straight, Mom letting me tell it all without interrupting. Then she smiled and said, "Good for her."

"I just thought you'd like to know," I said. "I

mean, we don't really have Mr. Lunn. Unless you want us to, that is."

Mom nodded. "It's not exactly the same situation, Jen, although you might think it is. You must remember that Mrs. Brandon's children still have their relationship with their father. Even though they're divorced they still see each other. You girls don't have that."

"So what? I only mentioned it because I thought you'd want to hear what Mrs. Brandon said. I liked that part about her trying to become her own person. I think that means you don't have to keep seeing Mr. Lunn strictly on our account."

Mom nodded gravely. "Thank you, Jenny. You've just struck another blow for Women's Lib."

"I did?"

Mom smiled. "Yes. Now go tell your sister we're eating early tonight."

I started off and then turned. "How come?"

Mom was sitting near the telephone, a strange smile on her face. "I'm going to try some of that nonsense you were telling me about."

I frowned. Dense. "What nonsense?"

"A life of my own."

CHAPTER 5

"GIRLS, this is Mr. Hart."

Chloris and I said hello when Mom introduced us. Mr. Hart was tall and thin with light blue eyes. He smoked a pipe and didn't have a beard.

"Hi," he said. Then, turning back to Mom, "Two of 'em, eh?"

Mom smiled sweetly and then told us we were excused. Chloris went back to her room and I followed. She bounced on her bed.

"What's going on?" she demanded. "What happened to Lunn?"

"I don't know," I said. "What do you think of this one?"

Chloris made a wry face. "Egh!"

"Anyway, he doesn't have a beard."

"At least he didn't try to get friendly," Chloris said. "That's something."

I decided I'd better tell her about Beverly's mother.

Chloris let her mouth hang open. "Four dates a week? She's got to be kidding! At her age?"

"That's what she told me," I said. "Anyway, she's not so old. She just got married early. That's why she has so many children."

Chloris couldn't get over it. "Four dates a week!"

I told her what Mrs. Brandon said about becoming her own person, then about keeping her children out of her affairs.

"Rotsa ruck," Chloris said.

"She said she didn't want people wandering in and out of their lives."

"Nobody's going to wander in and out of my life," she said fiercely.

"I just thought I'd tell you all about it so you'd be prepared."

"Don't worry about me," Chloris said. "I can handle it."

After Mr. Hart there was Mr. Swanson and then Mr. Sherry.

"That Mr. Swanson is too fat," Chloris said. "Also he chews gum. You have to be very careful of people who chew gum."

"How come?"

"It means they've got bad breath," she said.

"Mr. Sherry didn't chew gum."

Chloris shook her head. "We don't have to worry about Mr. Sherry. He doesn't stand a chance with Mom. He's too short."

"Why," I said. "Was Daddy . . . ?"

Chloris twisted her lip. "You know darn well he was tall. Don't pretend he wasn't. I'll tell you one thing. You sure have a rotten memory."

It sure *is* tough having a rotten memory. You feel like saying, "Hey, come on out. I know you're in there."

Grandma Grace had us over to her place for dinner a few days later. Grandma Grace is my Mom's mom. She lives alone. Grandpa Paul died before I was born so I never got to know him. She has a lot of pictures of him and he looked like a nice man.

I had a feeling that while my memory was kind of rotten Chloris' wasn't too reliable either, so after dinner, while Chloris was in the den watching TV I had a chance to ask, "Was my Daddy tall?"

Grandma looked at me. "Not particularly."

"About how tall was he?"

"Why do you want to know?" she asked.

I shrugged.

"He was about five eight or nine," she said. "About average height."

Chloris was watching the TV series with the genie when I told her. "Five eight or nine." She looked up at me frowning. "It's what Grandma just told me Daddy was."

Chloris nodded and turned back to the TV set. "Well, then, there you are. That's tall."

The next day during recess I asked Beverly Brandon how tall her father was.

"Six two," she said.

I didn't tell Chloris.

Friday night Mr. Lunn showed up again. He brought a box of candy for us.

"I'm not taking candy from that creep," Chloris said.

"How does giving us a box of candy make him a creep?" I asked. "Mr. Hart and Mr. Swanson and Mr. Sherry haven't brought us any."

"So what? They're creeps, too."

"I don't know," I said. "Anyway Mom now has her four dates just like Mrs. Brandon."

Chloris sniffed. "Big deal. What's that supposed to prove?"

"That she's popular?"

Chloris looked at me mean-eyed. "Nobody around here is asking her to be popular," she said angrily. "She's just supposed to be our mother. I don't need a lot of men coming around giving us candy."

"So far it's only been Mr. Lunn," I reminded her.

"You just wait and see," Chloris said. "I bet you if she keeps up with this mad dating plan of hers candy will be coming out of our ears."

I had the feeling she was right but I hated to admit it. "Maybe. Anyway, what's wrong with getting free candy? That way we don't have to spend any of our allowance money to buy it."

Chloris looked at me sadly and shook her head. "You don't understand anything, do you? Don't you know they're just trying to get on the good side of us?"

"What for?"

"So Mom will marry them. They're just trying to buy our affections."

"Maybe," I said. "But anyway so far it's only been Mr. Lunn."

"She'll have to do better than Mr. Lunn as far as I'm concerned. Nobody's buying my affections for a box of candy."

I noticed she was chewing and I looked down at the box. Almost the whole top layer of chocolates was gone.

"You're eating them anyway," I said accusingly.

Chloris turned up her nose. "I'm just helping out so you don't get sick eating them all by yourself. Don't you appreciate help?"

"Not that kind," I said.

Mr. Hart brought us a word game his next time over. You had to put your pieces on a board and spin a little wheel. Then a card of instructions told you from the number the wheel stopped at how many spaces you had to move up or down. I must have been lucky. In fifteen minutes I had all Chloris' pieces.

"I like this game," I said.

"Hart is a creep," Chloris said. "He's certainly not getting my affections buying me a game I lose at. He's probably a dumb businessman."

"Could be. Want to try another?"

"Uh-uh," said Chloris, shaking her head. "I've got better ways to spend my time."

"O.K., I'll play it with myself."

I played two more games using part of me as an imaginary other player and won both of them. I was sure hot that night. Mr. Hart left after a few more hours and Mom stepped into my room to make sure I was tucked in.

"That's a nice game Mr. Hart bought for us," I said.

"I'll tell him you liked it next time we talk."

"What do you think Mr. Swanson and Mr. Sherry will bring us?"

Mom straightened up, looking thoughtful. "I haven't any idea. They don't have to bring you anything, you know."

"I know," I said. "Are you going to meet any other new men?"

Mom blew out her cheeks and brushed a wisp of hair back from her forehead. "To tell you the truth, I don't know how Mrs. Brandon does it. I don't have the energy for all these people."

"Then how come you do it?"

Mom patted my head. "It seemed like a good idea at the time. Good night, pumpkin."

It was the first time she had called me that in a long time. It's a funny kind of nickname, one I never could figure out.

The following morning at breakfast, while Mom was in her room getting dressed for work, I told Chloris the news. "That game from Mr. Hart could be our last present."

Chloris looked at me questioningly. "How come?"

"Mom may be cutting down on her dates. She's getting tired. Running out of energy."

Chloris drained her milk glass and smacked her lips loudly. "It serves her right for going out with all those creeps. Creeps can drain all the energy out of a person."

"How?"

"Because they're so boring," Chloris said.

I didn't want to start an argument that early in the morning so I didn't press Chloris for a further explanation. She had this thing about creeps and nothing could change her mind. I tried to think of some people I didn't like but I didn't honestly think they were boring.

It was sad, I thought. Here was Mom all interested and excited in spending her spare time with new friends, then finding out she couldn't enjoy herself. I had heard that the older a woman got the less chance she had of getting married. I wasn't sure if this applied to those who were trying it for the first time, or the repeaters, like Mom, doing it all again. I supposed Mom knew that, too, and that was what was making her tired. I thought if I had to worry about it all the time it certainly would drain my energy. Like being turned down.

Probably the real reason for Mom's tiredness was getting depressed. I had the secret notion that she just couldn't go out on dates like Beverly's Mom, have a good time and a night out. Mom had something more important on her mind. Like getting herself a new husband.

A new father for her children.

I thought about the four men she had dated. Then all of a sudden I found that I had finally got myself depressed. I didn't really like any of them.

Not that much anyway. Not enough to want any of them to be my father.

Had Chloris come to this conclusion sooner because she was older and smarter? I thought some more and then decided that Chloris just didn't want *anybody* to be her new father. Mom could go out on a hundred different dates with a hundred different men and still my sister Chloris wouldn't like any of them.

Well, that's tough, I said to myself. If Mom found a nice man to be her husband I wouldn't mind. After all, I figured, what did I have to lose?

He might even be tall and handsome. Real tall.

At least six two.

CHAPTER 6

"WAIT till you see this one," Chloris said, a wicked glint in her eyes. "This one is old enough to be her father. She's got to be really scraping the bottom of the barrel now."

His name was Shepherd. I didn't ask if he got that name from somebody in his family tending sheep—I'm always curious about names—but this sheperd's face was very tan with a lot of wrinkles, especially when he laughed. The thick gray hair worried me because it meant Chloris was right and he was old—not old enough to be my grandfather exactly but a lot older than the fathers my friends had.

His eyes were a very deep blue with eyebrows dark and thick. He looked very rugged, almost handsome. *Anyway,* I thought, *Chloris can't call him a creep*. If any man looked positively uncreepy, that was Mr. Shepherd.

Mom still hadn't learned Beverly's mother's trick of keeping her new dates out of her children's lives. She introduced us to Mr. Shepherd.

He winked at me. "Hi. What's cooking?"

"Nothing," I said finally.

Mr. Shepherd nodded as if he was really interested in the fact that I didn't have anything cooking. His eyes shifted to Chloris who was wearing that same bored expression.

"I used to know an actress named Chloris," Mr. Shepherd said. "Are you going to be one, do you think?"

Chloris shrugged. "I don't know."

"Mr. Shepherd is a TV director," Mom said.

"Gy," I said. "What shows?"

He named one that Chloris and I used to watch.

"We don't see that one any more," I told him. "We have to be in bed by the time it now comes on."

"Oh?" he said. "Too bad." Then, "What's with that word 'Guy,' Jenny?"

Mom answered for me. "The kids use it nowadays the way we used 'Gee,' 'gosh' or 'golly.' They shortened it to Gy, pronounced Guy."

"Gy," he repeated, looking puzzled and not entirely happy with the feeling of it on his tongue.

Chloris looked at Mom. "Can we go to bed now?"

Mom was getting wise to Chloris. "Sorry to detain you," she said. "I didn't know you went to sleep at nine o'clock."

Chloris glared, got red in the face and stalked off.

"Good night," I said. "That was a pretty good show."

Mr. Shepherd smiled and said thanks.

I knew Chloris wasn't going to bed yet so I went into her room. She turned the TV set up louder. "Shut the door," she said. "I don't want to hear them getting mushy."

"What do you mean?"

Chloris looked down her nose at me. "Mushy. Don't you know what mushy means?" I shook my head dumbly. She cradled her arms and then rocked them the way you would rock a baby. Then she made a lot of kissing sounds and motions with her mouth. "That's what I mean about mushy."

I stared. I thumbed toward the closed door. "Mom and Mr. Shepherd?"

"You better believe it. Didn't you notice how giggly she was tonight? You watch and see. We're going to see a lot of Mr. TV Shepherd."

"Gy," I said. "Maybe he'll be able to give you a job in TV later on when you become an actress."

"Not me he won't. I wouldn't take a job if he offered it."

"Why not?"

Chloris glared at me and whispered, "Don't you understand *any*thing? He's trying to become our new father."

I didn't want to have Chloris get mad and throw me out of her room again, so I pretended I hadn't heard her.

"We already saw this show, remember? It's a repeat."

Chloris nodded. "That's why you have to watch

out for these creepy TV directors," she said.
"They try to cheat you." She tried a few other
stations but switched back. "Come to think of it,
I wasn't really listening last time. Once more
won't hurt."

I didn't argue and we sat back and watched it
together. Chloris acted as if she had never seen
this show before, laughing all the way through.
Then she played some of her records for me, and
hummed and laughed while the Beatles' music
filled her room. I started to yawn and think of
heading for my room. But Chloris kept pushing
and pulling, making me wrestle, and we did that
for a while. She won easily and after she let me up
asked if I wanted to hear any more records.

"Not tonight," I said. "I'm going to bed."

She looked disappointed, then shrugged and
bent down to her record player. I closed her door
when I went out. Mom and Mr. Shepherd were
still in the living room. I could hear their voices.
A few words from him, a few from her. Then a
lot of silence. The hi-fi in there was playing soft
music.

I had my light out when I heard a strange
sound. I opened the door and listened. It was
Chloris. Crying.

We found out one thing right away. If Mr.
Shepherd was going to marry Mom he wasn't worrying about us stopping him. He didn't waste his
time trying to buy our affections. He called for

Mom several times after that, and not once did he bring us a present. Not even a small one. Chloris had it figured out.

"He's just cheap," she said. "He's got his purse strings so tied up not even a nickel will fall out."

"Anyway," I said, "you can't say he's trying to bribe us. Into liking him, I mean."

Chloris tossed her head. "Don't kid yourself," she said. "He's just smarter than the others. He's got a different way to get what he wants."

I was mystified completely now. "I thought it depended on their bringing us presents. Now you're saying Mr. Shepherd is winning our affections a different way."

Chloris smiled thinly. "He only thinks he is. What he doesn't realize is, we're wise to him."

"Maybe you are. I'm not."

"You'll catch on," she said. "Just wait and see."

There wasn't anything else I could do.

As the weeks went by, Mom's dates all came around to bringing us girls something. Mr. Hart brought small fluffy stuffed animals. I got the goofy dog with the crossed eyes, after Chloris took the crocodile. "Cross him off the list," she told me.

Mr. Swanson brought jigsaw puzzles—an airport terminal and an atomic plant.

"Just what we needed," Chloris said. "We haven't even done the barnyard yet."

Mr. Sherry brought us each a small bicycle pump.

"Great!" Chloris said. "I haven't used my bike for years."

Mr. Sherry didn't know that. He had probably seen our bicycles outside and figured from the flat tires that we could use pumps. I didn't bother explaining.

Mr. Sherry, Mr. Swanson and Mr. Lunn kept bringing us things. About Mr. Lunn's giant lollipops. Chloris said, "He must have a brother who's a dentist." About Mr. Sherry's box of small flags of all nations, "I don't get it. What've these got to do with bicycle pumps?"

Chloris took out her list of names and what they had brought so far, adding the box of flags. And when Mr. Swanson next came to take Mom out bringing two more jigsaw puzzles—a circus and an aquarium—she tossed them carelessly on the floor in my room.

"He's got jigsaws on the brain," she said, putting them down on her list opposite Swanson's name. "He probably thinks he's developing our minds. All he's doing is giving me a headache thinking about putting those dumb things together."

I pointed to her list. "So far you don't have Mr. Shepherd down for anything."

Chloris pushed a wisp of trailing hair behind her ear. "He's just being careful. Biding his time. Waiting to see what the other guys do and then he'll come in with some whopping big one to make them all look cheap."

"I thought you said he was the cheap one."

"That's right," Chloris said. "So far he hasn't spent a dime, has he? Well, when he brings the big one, to zing the other guys, I'll bet you a quarter it'll be cheap. Big and cheap."

"I don't think so," I said.

Chloris grinned mockingly. "Want to bet?"

"No."

"Chicken," she said, walking away.

The next time I was invited over to my friend Beverly Brandon's house I looked carefully around. She had a large cheerful room. There were wide shelves on two walls completely covered with toys, and a small bridge table in one corner stacked with word games, all kinds of puzzles, paint boxes, and books. Along the bottom of the window wall there were little mechanical toys, cars, tractors, steam shovels, tanks, robots.

"You've got a lot of toys," I said.

"You think so?" Beverly said. "Look in here."

She led me to her closet. It was a long one with two sliding doors. She slid one door open. There were boxes of toys stacked up almost to my nose. She pointed up to the high shelf over the clothes pole. It was also crowded with boxes of toys.

"Wow!" I said.

Beverly grunted and pushed open the other sliding door. There were just as many boxes of toys on this side.

"You've sure got a lot of toys, Bev," I said, staring.

"I suppose so," she said. "But when my room gets too crowded we give a lot of them away to Goodwill."

"Did all these come from your mother's friends?" I asked.

Beverly shook her head, smiling. "Are you kidding? Most of them my Pop bought. And we've got a lot of relatives, you know."

"You mean he still gives you presents, even though you're divorced?"

"Of course," Beverly said. "What's that got to do with it? We still have a relationship, don't we?"

"Oh, yeah. I forgot."

Beverly is very sensitive. She must have noticed the look on my face. "By the way, how's your Mom doing?"

I shrugged. "Okay, I guess. She's dating four guys."

"Do you like any of them?"

"They're okay."

Beverly hit me on the arm. "You'll get used to it," she said laughing. "My Mom has dated a hundred of them."

"A hundred different men? Gy!"

Beverly grinned. "Well, not exactly a hundred, but a lot. You have to remember they've been divorced about five years."

"Doesn't he—I mean your father—mind?"

Beverly flopped over on her bed laughing. "Why should he? That was the whole idea, wasn't it?"

"What was?"

"Getting divorced. So they could lead their own lives."

CHAPTER 7

WE WAITED several weeks for Mr. Shepherd to show up again. Even Chloris, who hated to admit she was mystified, couldn't come up with a good guess. "Maybe he's more interested in dating actresses than working women. Maybe they dress better or something."

"Mom is a real neat dresser," I said. "She looks really great in that pink knit. It's just the right length."

Chloris pushed out her upper lip. She does this sometimes to give you the impression she's thinking. "Sure she does. I'm not saying she doesn't Although, maybe in a way, it's kind of too youthful for her. It's a little too much for a married woman with two children, don't you think?"

"How do you mean too much?"

Chloris put her hand down to her knee. "Too short. I think minis look better on younger women."

"Mom's not old," I said. "And anyway it's not a mini. It's just sort of high, that's all."

She shrugged. "That's what I mean."

"What about her blue cotton one? You said you liked that one on her. That's just as short."

Chloris shook her head. "Not exactly. I don't think so. Anyway, that's not the point. The point is Mom has to work for a living and those actresses Mr. Shepherd knows don't."

"You're crazy," I yelled. "They do too work. How do they get to be on TV if they don't work?"

"I mean in a store. There's a big difference, you know."

I couldn't think of an answer to that one, and Chloris walked off looking pretty smug, as if she had won the argument. The next time I had a chance I asked Mom directly.

"What happened to Mr. Shepherd?"

Mom looked up from her book. "What do you mean, what happened to him? Nothing's happened to him, so far as I know."

"I mean, he hasn't been around lately. You know."

Mom returned her attention to her book. With her eyes straight down on the page, she said, "Yes, Jenny. I know."

I stood closer, touching her shoulder. "Well, I mean, has anything happened? I mean, have you given up dating him?"

Mom closed her book. Then she leaned back on the sofa and closed her eyes. She looked tired. "There was nothing special about my relationship with Mr. Shepherd. I never told you that there was. He's a . . . well, he's a good friend."

I didn't like the way she said that. "I kind of

thought since you were dating, and all . . . ."

"We weren't exactly dating," Mom said, a tired smile on her face. "And it's not right for Mr. Shepherd and me to keep seeing each other. He's still married. Technically, that is. He's married legally even though he and his wife are separated."

"How can that happen?"

"His wife won't give him a divorce," Mom said.

"I thought everybody could get divorced now in California if they wanted to," I said.

"That's true, dear. But there has to be a settlement. And sometimes that can be very expensive."

"You mean a lot of money?"

"Sometimes an awful lot of money. And the house they live in. Sometimes it's easier to stay married than to get divorced and have no money to live on."

"Gy," I said, "that's not fair. Mr. Shepherd seemed like a nice guy."

Mom smiled a little easier this time. "Could it be you liked him because you learned he was a famous TV director?"

"Maybe. But he looked kind of nice. Even with the gray hair. Is he—very old?"

"Not particularly," Mom said. She sighed and looked at me very intently. "What's all this about?"

"I just thought everything was going to work out fine as soon as you used Mrs. Brandon's secret."

"It has," Mom said. "It's opened up my life. I'm having a very nice time. Going out once in a while with different people is fun."

I swung back to my subject. "But not if you can't go out and date whoever you want," I said. "I don't think it's fair for Mrs. Shepherd not to give her husband a divorce just because he's got a lot of money." I hesitated a second. Then, "Does he?"

Mom shrugged her shoulders. "I don't know. I haven't asked him." She shivered suddenly and her voice hardened. "It's not always women who are difficult and unreasonable about divorce. When I was married to your father I wanted a divorce, too, and he wouldn't give me one."

"But he must have," I protested. "Didn't you get divorced before he . . . before he . . ."

"Yes, eventually," Mom said wearily. "Many wasted years later."

"How come? What took so long?" I looked at her suddenly stricken by a new thought. "Was it because you wanted a lot of his money, too?"

Mom's laugh had a hollow sound. "No, it wasn't that. It was something you probably wouldn't understand, at all. It was because of you two girls. It's not the easiest thing in the world to break up a marriage when you have little children."

It didn't seem that difficult to me. "Why not?"

Mom sighed. "Because children need a father. A family."

"But you did . . . I mean, anyway you finally did get the divorce. Right?"

"Yes," she said, her voice low. "We finally agreed that it was for the best."

I wished I hadn't been so young when it all

happened. "How did you finally decide?" I asked.

Mom shook her head, smiled again, and reached up to pat my face gently. "You're asking too many questions for such a little girl. It's not something I like to talk about. We just decided that our marriage hadn't worked out. Not the way we originally thought it might. And so we ended it."

"And then Daddy got married again?"

Mom stiffened. I realized, now that it was too late, I shouldn't have said that. "Yes," she said dully.

I couldn't stop myself. "Why did he do it?"

Mom looked at me puzzled. "Do it? Do what?"

"You know. Kill himself."

Mom shook her head. Her eyes lifted to the opposite wall and stared. Her voice was very low. "Your father was a very unhappy man," she said finally.

"How come?"

She thought about it a little while. "For one thing, he had a very quick mind. And he liked quick answers, quick solutions. But things take a little longer than we want sometimes. He didn't have the patience to wait."

I couldn't imagine a person killing himself over that. "Like what, for instance?"

Mom shrugged. "He was always in a temper with his partners because they didn't do things his way—right away. They wanted to be sure of what they were doing . . . think things over. He was too impatient. That's one reason he changed his offices so many times. Now I'm not trying to say he was wrong about things. Only that he didn't have the patience to let things develop in their own time, their own way."

"Did Daddy make a lot of money?"

Mom smiled. "Not at first. But my father helped him get started. Paid our rent for a while, loaned us money so it took a lot of pressure off. And I worked for a few years—until Chloris and you were born. Then things got a little better for your father." She nodded her head, her eyes far away. "Yes, he made a lot of money, toward the end."

I couldn't remember any of that. I couldn't even remember where we had lived before this apartment house. "Do a lot of men do what he did? I mean . . . kill themselves because they make a lot of money and get too unhappy?"

Mom shook her head. "Not necessarily. Whatever gave you that idea?"

"Well, you said . . . ."

Mom leaned forward. "Just remember one thing, Jenny. Each person is different. People are different. Some take things easily. Some don't. Your father liked to have things his own way. The way he saw them. We didn't always agree. But that's only natural, you see. We were two different people. And, of course, he was a man and I a woman. Men and women don't see things the same way at all. They don't think alike either."

I threw in my usual, "How come?"

"Because they're different. You were very young

when we broke up, but you were certainly old enough when you visited with him on his boat to remember certain things about your father."

"Well, sort of," I said. "But it's like kind of mixed up."

She nodded thoughtfully. "I think perhaps that was the main tragedy with your father. The main reason he did what he did."

"You mean when he killed himself?" I didn't know why but I felt a slight shiver go right through me the moment I said the words.

"Yes. He was mixed up and he couldn't make up his mind."

"About what?"

"About me. About you girls. About some other women."

I stared up into Mom's eyes. For the first time, I was beginning to get the idea. Only I didn't like to come right out and say it.

Mom reached over and patted my hand. "You're a little young for this discussion. I'm afraid whatever I told you, you wouldn't really understand. You asked me a question and I'm trying to give you an honest answer. The trouble is . . . honest answers aren't easy. Perhaps we can talk about this another time, when you're a little bit older."

I shook my head stubbornly. I had a strong feeling that Chloris didn't have an idea at all of what Mom was telling me. That, for once, I was getting near to the truth.

"Maybe you can give me a little hint, then," I said.

Mom smiled. Her teeth are very large and white and, even though I look something like her, mine aren't nearly as white, and a whole lot more crooked. "It's not a new story to women," she said slowly. "A lot of women lose their men to other women." She looked guardedly into my face. "Are you sure you understand that?"

"Sure. Daddy went out with other women."

Mom sighed loudly. "I think that's enough for this session, Jen. Run along and do your homework."

"We don't have any today."

"Then read a book."

"But I read everything I have."

Mom looked at me, not cross exactly but as if I were giving her a pain she could do without. "How about doing your room then. And when you finish, you can mop the bathroom floor and do the tub and the basin."

I blew out my cheeks. "Gy, do I have to?"

She shrugged. "You don't seem to have anything else to do."

"I just remembered," I said. "Beverly asked me to call her up about a sleep-in party sometime soon."

"All right," Mom said. "Make your call."

I got up quickly and walked across the room toward the phone.

"When you're finished talking to Beverly," Mom said, "take out the garbage."

"It's Chloris' turn," I said.

"She's not here now. You are."

Some days you just can't win. Mom and I can have a perfect understanding, at times. Except when it comes to cleaning up my room, and the bathroom. Or taking out the garbage.

CHAPTER 8

Mr. Mancha. Fidel Mancha. Would you believe it? He's our new father!

He's a very big man with brown eyes and black hair mixed with some gray. His complexion is sort of brown, too, like he's tanned all over. He has a very wide chest and a big belly that swells out over his silver belt buckle. He is the happiest man I ever met. He is always laughing. When he isn't laughing, he sings or whistles.

I had heard some songs on my radio from a play called *The Man from La Mancha*. He was Don Quixote. Mr. Mancha laughed, shaking his big head, when I asked if there was any family connection.

"No," he said finally. "La Mancha is a place in Spain. If you are from there, you are called a *manchego*. I am from Guadalajara in Mexico. But I have been an American citizen many years. I am not anything like the brave Don Quixote, and I do not fight with windmills. There is plenty to fight without that."

Mom hadn't known Mr. Mancha for long, and

they had gone out only a few times. I didn't know they were in love or anything, so I was quite surprised when Mom broke the news. But while I was being just surprised Chloris practically flipped.

"But he's a Mexican," she said.

"Sure. So what?"

Chloris glared at me as if I had lost my senses. "Don't you understand, dumbbell? A Mexican."

"I know," I said. "He's also supposed to be a great artist."

She curled her lip. "How would you know?"

"Anyway, that's what Mom said."

It just shows how easy it is to get married and find a husband and a father for your two children all at the same time. Mom took a stroll one Monday evening along La Cienega Boulevard. There are a lot of big restaurants on the street and a lot of art galleries. People walk it more on Monday nights when most of the new art shows open to the public.

Mom walked smack into the gallery that was exhibiting Mr. Mancha's paintings and sculpture pieces. She liked everything she saw, she said. Mr. Mancha was there, too, as most of the artists are at opening nights of their exhibitions. They got talking to each other about this and that, according to Mom, and discovered they had a lot in common. According to Mom, she didn't think about him being Mexican, one way or the other. All she saw was a very talented, big-hearted, good-natured human being. She found out he was a widower, and he found out she was a divorcee, and that was the beginning of everything.

Chloris was kind of sarcastic about it. "That's the kind of luck we have," she said. "If she had walked on the other side of Cienega she might have married a Chinaman."

"How come?"

She tossed her head. "They probably give one side of the street to the Mexicans and the other to the Chinamen."

"So what? We're supposed to be friendly with the Chinese now, aren't we? The President said it was okay."

Chloris stared at me. "Are you for real?" she demanded. "For a *father?*"

It's probably a good thing Mom didn't hear that. At school we don't have any Chinese boys or girls, but we have a few *Chicanos* and several blacks. One of the blacks in my class, Hugo Charles, is considered quite a gifted artist by our teacher. In the class above mine, the fourth, there are two *Chicanos,* Mexican-Americans. One is very tall and a good runner. The other is short and I've seen him smoking outside of school with some other kids.

Mr. Mancha is very easy to talk to and one day I asked him how come there were so few *Chicanos* at school, and what did they do to get out of it. Mr. Mancha explained that most black and browns were poor and couldn't get good jobs. That was why they couldn't afford to live in good neighborhoods like ours and go to our good school.

"This is a very good country," he said, "but some people are not so lucky. To be born the wrong color is a big mistake."

"But that's not fair," I said. "They can't help it."

Mr. Mancha smiled.

"Those people are probably just as good as we are."

He reached down and patted my hair. "Probably."

"So, how come?"

"Don't forget the Indians," Mr. Mancha said. "I think maybe they are even worse off."

"That's different," I said. "Indians used to scalp people. They attacked our wagon trains. They scalped all the helpless women and children."

Mr. Mancha looked puzzled. "Where did you hear that?"

"I saw it myself on TV," I told him.

Mr. Mancha nodded and pursed his lips and didn't say anything. He didn't seem convinced. He's probably so busy painting pictures that he never gets a chance to watch TV and you can miss a lot that way. I've probably seen over a hundred Indian massacres already and I'm only eight years old.

I didn't want to hurt Mr. Mancha's feelings, but I've seen a lot of Mexicans killing and shooting up our womenfolk and their children on TV too. And I've never seen even one episode where we whites shoot up and kill a lot of innocent Mexican women and children, especially when their men-folk are away someplace.

I couldn't see Mr. Mancha doing a thing like that, though. For one thing, he's too gentle even if he is so big. And then, he's always laughing.

CHAPTER 9

IT WAS decided we would move into Fidel Mancha's house.

"How come?"

"He has his studio there, dear. It's where he works. It's a very big house with enough room for everybody."

It was in Tigertail Canyon off a winding dirt road halfway up a hill surrounded by mountains. There were other houses in the area, some perched on top of the crestline, others under the rim snuggled among the trees and rocks. The air was clean and fresh, mixed with strange flower and grass odors. Although only about fifteen minutes from where we lived before, Tigertail Canyon was like living in the country. Wild flowers grew all around the big wood-sided sprawling house Mr. Mancha worked and lived in. Tiny humming birds hung in the air sucking at the nectar in the Jack-in-the-pulpits, their wings beating so fast you couldn't see them move. Bees were attacted, too.

Fidel explained how I should behave near bees so they wouldn't get nervous or frightened and sting me. I was to stand or sit perfectly still, not get excited and wave my arms around. Not scream or run or strike at them if they happened to be cruising around or even settling on me. He said they were attracted by loud colors. Most of the time they would mistake me for a flower if I was wearing something bright, and not really mean anything by buzzing me. It was easier to wear drab clothes rather than to keep holding my breath worrying if the bees understood Fidel's rules about living peacefully with bees.

Chloris pretended she didn't need his advice. "I'm not changing my habits for a lot of dumb bees."

After a few large bumblebees gave her their special buzz-down treatment and chased her off screaming she caught on. "I'm wearing these old jeans and this brown shirt today because it fits my mood," she would say casually. "I happen to be depressed, if you want to know."

I counted at least eleven rooms in the house. They were at different levels, running up and down to fit the side of the hill. The living room had a fireplace big enough to roast a bear. We had never before had a real fireplace and I couldn't wait to sit before the fire at night and toast marshmallows and stare at the leaping flames.

Fidel and Mom had the front bedroom upstairs. It had a huge fireplace, too. Chloris and I had our own rooms, as before, next to each other. The hills behind us cut off the night wind, so we didn't need a fireplace.

"It figures," Chloris said. "We're only kids so they take the room with the best view."

I didn't mind. You could look out the bedroom windows and watch the soft purple light of dusk deepen into night. Suddenly the mountain became invisible. It was right there but you couldn't see it. The crickets kept sounding off all night and early at sunrise birds started saying good morning to each other.

"Quiet!" Chloris would scream. "I'm trying to sleep, you dopes!"

Once in a while I would look up and see a deer posed on the hill. Standing absolutely motionless as if thinking about something. Wondering maybe if she was lost and, if this were really the country, what were all those houses doing around? The next moment, I would blink in surprise. The deer had silently disappeared. For no good reason, seeing one always made me sad.

I didn't see any barnyard animals but there were plenty of dogs around. Nights, they bayed at the moon. One would howl to start it off. Another farther away heard the message and started to howl, too. Soon there would be a whole chorus of dog music lasting far into the night.

"That's just great," Chloris would say. "Now we're living in a stupid jungle. Next thing you know, we'll be invaded by elephants."

The kitchen downstairs was large and always splashed with sunshine. Whoever built it had been very smart about putting it there so the mountain behind couldn't cut off the morning sun. Other rooms would be in shadow early in the day and then get the afternoon light. But I think nothing is as important really as having a cheerful kitchen in the morning.

Fidel's studio was a big barnlike wing attached to the side of the house. It looked like the world's biggest indoor junkyard. There were about a million pieces of junk. Metal scraps, boxes, wires, rocks, shells, broken clocks, and motor parts. A lot of rusted metal that looked to be farm machinery. It all was heaped over big tables, hung on walls, littered the wooden floor. Canvasses were piled in the corners. Some were finished paintings that blazed with color. Others had been started and set aside. There were big objects nailed and assembled together looking strange and almost frightening. Fidel called these his sculpture constructions. He made them out of the junk that cluttered his studio.

At first it looked like Fidel was the world's sloppiest artist. Then I saw how he used that junk. He cut it into the shapes he wanted with hacksaws. He broke big planks apart with a heavy sledgehammer. He banged things together with long nails, or cemented them with oozing melted lead and a blowtorch. When he was finished he had made something nobody else in the world would have thought of. It was as if he were redesigning the world.

I asked him, "How come you make everything out of junk?"

Fidel stopped hammering. He patted the gigantic thing he had made affectionately with his big hands.

"It pleases me," he said, "to make something beautiful out of pieces of scrap. Everything here has been used some time and then discarded. I give it another chance now to be something. What it becomes does not matter. Whether it is art does not matter. What is important is that I am using the imagination God gave me, to shape things with my two hands."

"Do people buy those things?"

Fidel laughed. "Sometimes. Some things I make for myself. Just for the fun of making them."

I looked around the room slowly at all the things he had fun making. It seemed like a lot of work. "But don't you lose money that way?"

He nodded. "Perhaps. But money is not my God, you see. An artist must create for the sheer joy of creating. That is worth much more than the money."

I wondered what I might have made with any of that junk strewn all over his large studio. I could imagine some fun hammering the big nails into wood, but I couldn't see what would happen after that. "How can you tell if you're going to be an artist?"

Fidel thumped his wide chest with one big fist. "In here. It tells you."

I wanted to thump my own chest to find out but I didn't. I could tell right away I wouldn't get that same deep sound.

Fidel must have read my mind. He smiled broadly. "Some day I will let you try the blowtorch. It might frighten you but then you would like it."

He picked up part of a hose and flicked the end. A long ribbon of blue fire ran out. I jumped.

Fidel laughed.

He made toys, too. Like everything he made, they were giant-size. He had made a hobby horse that was at least ten feet tall, the head alone bigger than I was. But when he picked me up and sat me on it, I had the weirdest feelings. First I felt very peaceful. Then I imagined the big strange-looking horse underneath me, made of huge beams and covered with scraps of leather, suddenly coming to life, covering the world in giant bounds, swooping up to the sky, carrying me with it.

I got so excited I nearly fell off. Can you imagine falling off a wooden horse that isn't even moving?

I told Chloris about the wooden horse, even dared her to get up on it. She sniffed.

"That's all I need. What a big thrill that would be. Me sitting up there on that creepy thing." She stared up at it. "It doesn't even look like a horse. It doesn't look like anything. Except maybe a lot of junky wood."

Another thing Chloris didn't like was the way Fidel spoke. His sentences were like a running tune. It was like he was singing when he talked. When he wasn't around, she mimicked him, making him sound very Spanish or Mexican. "Some father she picked for us," she said sarcastically. "Next thing you know, I'm going to flunk my best subject—English."

She didn't like the way he was built, either.

"He's too fat. He ought to go on a diet. Can you imagine *our* Daddy going around looking that way?"

"What way?" I asked.

She leaned back pushing out her stomach, looking pregnant. "This way."

"Maybe he can't help it. Maybe he's that way because he's so good natured."

"Big deal," Chloris said.

"You mean our Daddy didn't have a . . . a belly?"

Chloris shook her head, her lips set primly. "No way," she said. "He looked like an athlete."

Darn, I thought. *I couldn't even remember that.*

I heard a deep noise roaring in my ears. It bubbled higher and higher. The more I heard it, the nicer it sounded.

It's okay. That's Fidel laughing.

My own jigsaw puzzle. What was my Daddy like?

Is that important? I wondered.

It's got to be, I told myself fiercely, *if Chloris and I have different ideas about what he was like.* It was like having two different answers to the same puzzle. Like forcing pieces to fit that really didn't.

Mom didn't like to talk about him. Grandma Grace didn't seem too happy being reminded of him, either. Well, they were mother and daughter, and it was natural for them to be on the same side.

Grandma Helen was too far away to ask. Besides, she was too prejudiced. You could tell she liked everything about her son. And even young as I was, I knew it was wrong for her to be telling Chloris all that jazz about how it was Mom's fault for him killing himself.

How could it be her fault?

How could anybody make somebody else do a thing like that?

Maybe Mom's story was nearer the truth. That he was so mixed up that he couldn't think straight. It seemed to me that a person would have to be awfully mixed up to do a thing like that.

What really happens when you die? I wondered.

Does anybody really know?

And if you don't know for sure how can you do a thing that is so final and definite. I mean, after you do a thing like that, after you get it started and start dying, you can't say, hey, wait, I didn't mean it, I want to think this thing over . . .

I thought of Mrs. Brandon and her husband and how they just decided to break it up and live their own lives. That seemed like a sensible solution. Why couldn't Daddy have done a simple thing like that?

Was it to blame her, maybe? Make her seem guilty?

Gy, what did she ever do to him?

Then I had the opposite answer. That if he was mixed up, then naturally she wouldn't have had to do anything to him. It would be all in his own head. All mixed up.

Like Chloris was.

I sat up in bed, suddenly feeling excited.

That's it, of course. She's all mixed up.

I tried to remember if things like that were supposed to run in the same family.

I thought so hard about it, I fell asleep.

In the morning, I heard Mom busy downstairs cooking breakfast. I could smell the nice breakfast aroma of bacon and eggs and coffee. Then I heard hammering. Mixed in with the hammering was singing.

That would be Fidel. Working already on another creation.

Making something nice again out of some of his junk.

I got up quickly and got dressed. I could hardly wait to see it. On the way downstairs, I was struck with another thought. When Fidel died, he would leave a lot of his things around and people could tell from them pretty much what he was like.

Our Daddy didn't leave us anything.

I would always remember Fidel from his hearty laugh, the easy good-natured bearlike manner he had. It seemed nothing could possibly upset him.

Even without his paintings and his big way-out constructions, he left a lot to be remembered by.

Now Daddy on the other hand . . .

Forget it, I told myself, *your breakfast will be getting cold.*

CHAPTER 11

THE school bus rolled through the twisting turns of Tigertail Canyon bringing us back home. Though it wasn't so easy seeing Beverly Brandon at her house any more we kept up our friendship in school.

"How are you doing," she asked now. "What's happening?"

I told her about Fidel Mancha and everything.

Beverly's eyes glowed. "Gy, that sounds terrific, Jen. Tell him my dad is very rich. Maybe he can sell him something."

"I don't know," I said. "His stuff is pretty big. It fits okay in his studio, but that's as big as a barn. I don't see how any of his work could fit into somebody's house."

Beverly thought about it for a sec. "No problem. Just tell him to saw them in half. That way you could even get it in two rooms."

I told her I would speak to Fidel about it.

"How does your sister like him?"

I didn't know what to say or how much Beverly knew about our personal problem. Finally I said,

"She hasn't exactly made up her mind yet."

But she had, of course. She had it made up long before she ever met Fidel Mancha.

He was good-natured but he wasn't dumb. It didn't take him long to catch on that he was getting the cold treatment. It must have puzzled him at first. I overheard him speaking to Mom one evening not long after we had moved into his house.

"Why doesn't that one like me?"

Mom's tone was bitter. "She doesn't like me, either. Not since I divorced my husband. But it became worse after he killed himself."

Mr. Mancha was silent for a while. "Don't worry," he said at last. "She will come around. She is too young to keep such a hate bottled up inside her."

I shook my head. He might be a good artist but he sure didn't know the first thing about Chloris.

Fidel kept on acting as if he didn't know a thing one way or the other. He always treated me with affection, and he didn't change any for Chloris. Whatever he offered me he offered her. She would back off, or pretend she wasn't interested, or that she was too busy, or too tired, or too this or that. Fidel didn't seem to mind. He would nod, his brown eyes soft and understanding. Then he would laugh.

"Okay. We'll forget it for now."

I spoke to Fidel about Beverly's suggestion.

"He is rich, her father, you say?"

"Oh, yes. Beverly says he's very rich. He lives in

Beverly Hills." I suddenly wondered if that's how my friend Beverly got her name by being born there. I made a mental note to ask her about it.

Fidel shrugged his heavy shoulders. "My work is at the galleries. If he likes something there, he can buy it. We don't pick out favorites to buy our things."

I had never been down to his exhibit gallery. "Is it the same kind of work you have here in your studio?"

"Pretty much. Perhaps now I am working a little bit larger."

"That's it!" I cried.

I passed on Beverly's suggestion about cutting his things in half if they were too big for the average house to hold.

Fidel looked thoughtful. "I never thought of that," he said. "Now I can make twice as much money from the one thing."

"How come?"

"Simple. I cut it in half and sell two of them."

Then he patted me on the head and started to laugh.

Sometimes I thought Fidel didn't take me seriously.

He was quite serious about our safety, though.

"Be careful, girls, when you walk in the hills. There are rattlesnakes in there."

Chloris looked at me and winked. I looked back at Fidel.

"Are you sure?"

He nodded, his face serious. "Under dead wood. Under logs or rocks. Snakes like to keep cool. Be very careful."

Chloris laughed. She acted pretty brave about it. "Don't worry," she said smiling. "We won't step on any."

Fidel watched us go outside, his eyes worried.

The ground around Fidel's house sloped up gradually at first, then became steep. We had to walk around thick wiry little bushes. There were lots of little stones and sometimes when our feet hit one of them they would all start rolling down.

"Where are we going?" I asked when we were about halfway up the mountain. Chloris pointed ahead to the crest. It looked like a tough hard climb. I was tired already. "Don't forget what Fidel said. What about the rattlesnakes?"

Chloris snickered. "Do you believe everything that creepy Fidel tells you?"

"Sort of," I said. "Especially about rattlesnakes."

Chloris smiled and whacked at a bush. "You'll believe anything you hear. Do you see any snake down there?"

I held my breath. Then I let it out, relieved.

"Come on, silly," Chloris said.

She stepped over a rotted dead log, beckoning me to follow. Her hind foot slipped and her lead foot hit the log making it roll back. Chloris caught her balance and started up again.

"Somebody ought to clean up this stupid jungle," she said. Then she stopped.

I heard the sound at the same time.

It was coiled in a big circle of brown and white spots, its tiny triangular head sticking out. The strange sound came again and I watched its tongue flick out.

"Come on. Run."

I reached my hand up to her. She shook her head. Her face was pale, her mouth open, her eyes fixed on the snake.

"I . . . I c-can't . . ."

She started to tremble all over, shaking as if she were having a fit. That scared me almost as much as the snake.

"Maybe it won't follow us," I said. "Come on. Let's run."

She shook her head, her throat taut trying to swallow, her eyes still on the snake as if she were hypnotized.

I heard a shout behind me and heavy breathing. Fidel loomed suddenly at my side. He brushed me back easily with one hand. I pointed down at the rattler and he nodded without saying anything to me, but he spoke sharply to Chloris.

"Step aside."

She acted as if she didn't hear. Her chest was going up and down like crazy, a strange sound coming from her throat.

Fidel stepped forward and grabbed her arm. Her mouth jerked open wider but she didn't look at him or say anything. He yanked her back almost off her feet. As her heels skidded on the dirt, suddenly the snake moved, its coils opening as it started to slither off. Fidel raised his arm.

I hadn't even seen the axe in his hand. He swung it down quickly and I heard the thud and saw the blade bite through the snake's body into the ground. Fidel leaned down and then threw the thick and wiggling thing in his hand in a high arc far up the mountain. I followed its path until it landed away out of sight. When I looked back at the ground I saw the rest that Fidel had chopped off, the motionless head and the gaping wound.

I still couldn't say anything. Chloris swayed, her face paler even than before. As she fell back, Fidel caught her with one arm. He looked down at me, his eyes puzzled.

"I told you both it was dangerous up here. That there are snakes. Why didn't you believe me?"

I shook my head. I looked down at the redness around his axe blade, tried to catch my breath, to talk. I felt awfully tired.

"I don't know," I said.

He looked deep into my eyes, his face quiet. Then he swung Chloris under his arm as if she weighed maybe a pound. He jerked his head downward toward the house.

"Let's go, then. All right?"

I ran down the hill without stopping, making a lot of those bushes sorry they were in my path, Fidel close behind with Chloris tucked under his arm. The big axe swung easily in his other hand. No other snakes came out to bar our passage.

I opened the screen door and Fidel carried Chloris through, her eyes closed, her body limp, up to her room and on to her bed. He went out for a moment and came back with a wet towel from the bathroom. He folded it on her forehead. Then he checked the pulse of her right wrist.

"She'll be all right," he said softly and left.

In a little while Chloris opened her eyes. She stared vacantly at the ceiling and shivered, then reached up and touched the towel on her head. She picked it off and looked at it.

"What's all this?" she asked.

I told her how Fidel came up the hill in time and chopped the snake in two with his big axe and threw it away up the hill. "You fainted, it looked like, and he carried you down. I guess Fidel saved our lives."

Chloris thought about it. Her tongue licked at her dry lips. She took a deep breath, then surprised me by smiling.

"Daddy wouldn't have needed an axe. Daddy would have killed that old rattlesnake with his bare hands."

I started to say something. Chloris stared back defiantly, daring me to say it.

I couldn't think of a thing to say.

CHAPTER 12

WHEN Mom came from work, I told her about the snake. She shuddered. "It would have scared me to death. Lucky for us all that Fidel was there."

"You can say that again," I said. Chloris didn't care to talk about it. From the way she acted, you would never guess Fidel had saved her life. He seemed to ignore what happened, too, as if it weren't any more difficult than banging those big nails into his wooden statues. He cleaned the blood off the axe, put it away, and went back to his studio and his work.

He and Mom must have had a discussion that night. She called Chloris and me together, and when he left the room she began. "Girls, Fidel is now your new father and . . .

Chloris interrupted. "I don't want a new father."

Mom looked down at her fingernails. "Nevertheless, you now have one. Fidel likes you both and wants to adopt you legally."

"What does that mean?" I asked.

"It's done through the courts. You will become

his daughters legally. He will give you his name and be responsible for you."

"What does that mean?" I asked again.

"It means you both will be legally protected by his estate. Whatever money he leaves. It could help put you through college. Your name would be changed to Jennifer Mancha."

It had a nice sound as I thought about it. I said okay.

Mom turned to Chloris. "Do you have any questions?"

Chloris shrugged and looked away. "Nope."

Mom sighed as if with relief. "That's fine. Just give him a chance, and you'll see we'll all be happy. He really is a very nice man. He's also a very gifted artist and sculptor. You girls will be proud when he gets the recognition he deserves."

Later I asked Chloris about that recognition business.

"It means he's nobody now and maybe he will be somebody some time. If he's lucky. If he lives long enough. Like that."

"Maybe he'll be lucky."

"Sure," Chloris said. "That will be the day." She hugged herself fiercely. "It will also be the day when I let that fat creep adopt me and give me his name. Can you imagine—Chloris Mancha?" She made a wry face. "It makes me sound like *him*."

"You wouldn't have wanted any of the others for your last name, either," I pointed out. "Lunn, Hart, Sherry, Swanson, or Shepherd."

Chloe narrowed her eyes. "Right on. My name is Chloris Carpenter. My real name. Yours is Jenny Carpenter." Her hazel eyes became slits. "You got that? Jenny *Carpenter!*"

A few weeks later a lady called at our house. She said her name was Mrs. Lindsay and she was a social worker from the Court. She spoke with Mom and Fidel for a while. Then they left the room and she signalled for us to come in.

"I have two girls of my own," she said as we entered the living room. "Almost your ages." She motioned to the chairs around the big table for us to sit down and join her. "How old are you?" she asked Chloris.

"Eleven. Halfway to twelve," Chloe said.

Mrs. Lindsay looked thoughtful and wrote something on a sheet of paper. "Under the new law," she explained, "twelve-year-olds have the right to determine for themselves whether or not they want to get adopted, or to have their names changed legally."

"I'm only eight," I said.

Mrs. Lindsay smiled. "Eights don't cut any ice." She turned to Chloris. "Since you will be twelve soon we try to make some allowance for that. To ask your own preference. You can speak freely. Whatever choice you make will be written down as yours. I may indicate my own judgment in my statement to the Court, but your own decision will go on the record. Do you understand?"

Suddenly I felt very nervous. My legs began to

itch and I had to scratch, even if Mrs. Lindsay noticed and put it down on the record. Chloris, sitting next to me on the opposite side of the table from Mrs. Lindsay, nodded and then yawned.

"My name is Chloris Carpenter," she said stonily.

Mrs. Lindsay looked down at her hand holding the pen on the long white sheet of paper. "You're telling me you don't want your name changed. Is that correct?"

"Correct."

"How do you feel about Mr. Mancha adopting you as his legal daughter?"

"Forget it," said Chloris.

Mrs. Lindsay bent her head and wrote something down. "How do you feel about Mr. Mancha? Do you like him?"

Chloris shrugged. "He's okay, I guess. Mom picked him. Do I have to like him?"

Mrs. Lindsay smiled thinly. "No, dear. I'm here to ask your own preference so that we can record it for the court."

"Okay. So I told you." Chloris drummed her fingers on the table.

Mrs. Lindsay was looking at me, smiling, her head cocked. "What about you, Jennifer? How do you feel about Mr. Mancha?"

"He's okay," I said. "I guess," I added.

I couldn't believe it but that's what I was saying.

"How do you feel about being adopted by Mr. Mancha and having your name changed to Jennifer Mancha?" she asked.

I heard my voice, very weak, as if from a great distance. "No," it said. "No, thanks. My name is Carpenter. Jenny Carpenter."

I looked quickly at Chloris. *Thanks,* her eyes said.

Waiting in the other room with Chloris, I heard the hurt surprise in Fidel's voice.

"They turned me down? Both of them?"

Mrs. Lindsay murmured something softly. I guessed she was telling him that was exactly what happened, sir.

"I can't believe it," Mom said. "Jenny sided with her sister?"

"Yes," Mrs. Lindsay said. "But in my experience, Mrs. Mancha, that isn't too unusual. Siblings tend to stick together in these situations."

"I'm terribly sorry, Fidel," Mom said. "I had no idea. When I proposed the idea, both girls appeared to accept your adopting them."

"If it's any comfort, Mr. Mancha," the lady social worker said, "I am still going to recommend the adoption to the Court."

"What good is that?" he said softly. "It's clear they do not want it themselves."

"It will be up to the judge at the hearing," she said. "He makes the final decision, and I feel certain it will be in favor."

Chloris was clutching my arm, her face screwed up as she tried hard not to miss a word. "Did you hear that?" she whispered fiercely in my ear. "The creep!"

"Thank you very much," Fidel was saying, "but the decision has already been made. I would not go against the girls' wishes in this matter. So I will drop the idea."

Chloris breathed a huge sigh of relief. She hammered me on my back jubilantly. "There you are," she said. "Saved!"

It wasn't all over yet, however. Mom came and told us Mrs. Lindsay wanted to talk to us again. Chloris put on a weary expression.

"What? Again?"

I didn't say my usual *How come?* I felt too ashamed to look at Mom as we walked past. Mrs. Lindsay gestured to the chairs again.

"Sit down, girls."

Chloris stared at her stubbornly without moving. Mrs. Lindsay pretended to be busy with the papers in front of her and didn't repeat her order. She slumped in her chair, elbows on the table, her head in her hands, as if worn out after a hard day's work. Mrs. Lindsay looked up, nodded and didn't say anything. She fussed with her papers for a while longer, giving Chloris a chance to rub her nose, scratch her ear, and pull up her socks. I was so busy watching Chloris I didn't have a chance to act nervous.

Mrs. Lindsay cleared her throat. "I must tell you that even though both you girls are against being adopted by Mr. Mancha, I approve of it."

Chloris sat up straighter, warily eyeing Mrs. Lindsay.

"It would mean a happier family, girls, believe

me," Mrs. Lindsay continued. "We've had a lot of experience in these matters. Therefore, in my report to the Court, I am going to recommend the adoption, as originally requested."

Chloris looked at her, a little frightened. "But he said . . . I mean . . . does that mean he can still adopt us? Even if we both don't want to be?"

Mrs. Lindsay turned from Chloris to me. "That will be up to the judge at the hearing. He will consider all the facts and the final decision will be his."

Chloris didn't like that but she must have sensed that this Mrs. Lindsay was a tough cookie, so she didn't argue. Instead, she showed Mrs. Lindsay her sweet helpless expression, as if to show how willing she was to cooperate, even if it killed her.

"That's all, girls. Thank you. And I hope you both will be happy."

Chloris didn't say anything. I wanted to, but couldn't find words, except finally, " 'Bye." I followed Chloe as she ran up the steps to her room. She surprised me by running on ahead and shutting the door behind her.

I went into my own room and stared out the window. It was just around dusk and the mountain was beginning to change color. I could hear a few crickets warming up. Then some night birds started to call to each other, asking everybody around how they were and all, and answering back. There was a lot to chirp about. There were long sentences and short. Happy trills.

I became aware of a louder more persistent noise. It came on steadily, almost without pause. I should have known sooner that it was Fidel back in his studio, hammering away at some new piece of sculpture. Tonight he seemed to be hitting harder than ever. I felt a little bit sorry for those long nails.

I opened my window a little more so that I might be able to see a deer if one came by. Mrs. Lindsay came out the screen door beneath my window and then Mom, talking in a low voice, explaining her main reason for wanting Fidel to adopt us. It turned out to be another reason than the one she gave us. It concerned Grandma Helen in Cleveland. Daddy's mother. The one who tried to brain-wash us that night.

"I absolutely detest that woman," Mom was saying. "She ruined her son the way she brought him up. Making him absolutely dependent so that he couldn't handle any situation by himself. I wanted Fidel to adopt the girls in case something were to happen to me. I didn't want that woman to get her hands on them to poison their minds against me, as she already has."

Mrs. Lindsay listened. "I'm almost certain the adoption would be approved by the Court if you could persuade your husband to change his mind."

Mom shook her head. Her voice was bitter. "How could I ask him to do that after they rejected him. The judge at the hearing might turn him down anyway. He might not like Mexicans. That would give Chloris another triumph. No dear. I don't think we should risk giving her that kind of satisfaction. I'll go along with his decision now and we'll withdraw the application. Thank you for everything."

It was the first time I ever really felt like a creep!

CHAPTER 13

A FEW days later we got an invitation in the mail —from Mrs. Cindy Carpenter! A birthday party for her son Jeff. On the opposite side of the announcement part she had written. *Dear Chloris and Jennifer—I wonder if you would like to come to your half-brother's party. He will be three years old. But I have two other children nearer your age and it might be fun and anyway nice to meet your relations. If your mother agrees, I will be very happy to pick you up in time and bring you home.*

I expected Mom would blow a fuse but she merely told us we could go if we wanted to. That it was strictly up to us.

I looked at Chloris. She gave me her I-don't-care shrug, so I said okay. I wondered what Daddy's little boy looked like. If it resembled Daddy, maybe then I'd have a better idea of what he looked like. I pointed to the signature on the card.

"How come her name is the same as ours?"

"He married her, didn't he?" Mom said. "She

took his name in marriage. Just as I did."

"But I heard he left her and . . ." I stopped confused.

"Left," Mom said. "Not re-married." She smiled slightly at me. "Besides, he left me and did remarry, and I still used his name. I'm his ex-wife and Cindy was his last wife. Understand?"

"Just barely," I said. Actually, I wasn't even that close. But I didn't want to ask any more questions because I know that topic isn't Mom's favorite.

Saturday morning a horn honked outside and Cindy was there in a red Toyota. Mom had Chloris and me ready, all dressed up nice, even presents from us for Cindy's son. She didn't come out to talk to Cindy or wish her a happy birthday for Jeff. I kind of wished she had, but then I'm not a divorced woman.

Cindy lived in West Los Angeles, not too far from where we used to live. Her apartment looked something like the one we had, too. I nudged Chloe. "The furniture looks nice," I said, holding this observation down to a whisper. "Almost like ours."

Chloris gave me her superior look. "Of course, dumbbell. Daddy bought it. He had a lot of money, you know. And he wasn't cheap about spending it."

I suddenly realized he must have had a lot of money. Because not only was he then paying us alimony but he had to support Cindy after he married her.

My next surprise was meeting Cindy's other children. The boy Lester was a year younger than Chloe but a little taller. He wasn't too bad-looking for that age. Her daughter Lucy was two years younger than I, her hair already almost as long as mine. I didn't care too much for that. Mine could have been longer if I'd started letting it keep on growing sooner. But I was taller than she, so that was something.

Little Jeff wasn't able to talk much but he smiled a lot. It was hard to tell if he looked like Daddy because he didn't have any teeth. His hair was black. He had brown eyes and a little nose. Not pointed.

The other kids started arriving and put down their presents. It was a pretty good party. Cindy had name cards for us at the table and we played a lot of games and all sat around clapping when she opened Jeff's presents. She thanked each one as she read the card and showed the present. We brought Jeff a little sailor hat and a furry toy animal called a Panda.

In a couple of hours we were all pretty worn out from having to sing all those songs and play all those games. We all had tried hard not to have any arguments about anything and it was quite a strain. Soon afterward, parents started calling for their kids. When we were about the last left I started looking around. Cindy saw me and came over.

"Do you want the bathroom?" she whispered.

"Not exactly. I mean, no thanks," I said.

She looked puzzled. I noticed now she was looking less like the secretary she always used to look like and more like a harried housewife.

"I just wondered if you had any pictures around of my . . . uh . . . Daddy."

Her lips dropped apart. "You mean you don't have any?" I started to shake my head and feel sorry for myself all of a sudden. She snapped her fingers and said, "Of course. Naturally. I can't say that I blame your mother." I wondered what that was all about. Then she said, "We don't have any pictures of your father here, either. You know he left us, don't you?"

I hesitated. "Well . . . kind of . . ."

She frowned. "There wasn't any 'kind of' about it. He left us. Left us before his son was even born. How about that?"

I couldn't tell her. I had enough trouble feeling sorry for myself without worrying about her kid.

"What about Lucy and Lester," I asked, changing the subject. "Is their father . . . I mean . . . did he . . . ?"

Cindy looked down at me without too much friendliness showing. "Did he what—shoot himself or divorce me? Is that your question?"

"I guess. Something like that."

Her tone was flat. "He's still alive somewhere. We were divorced, a long time ago. He never could hold a job." She looked sharply at me. "Why do you think I worked for your father?"

I couldn't answer that one, either. I just looked up at her hoping she didn't tell everybody around how dumb I was.

"I took the job because I needed money to support my kids," Cindy snapped. As if it were my fault.

I looked around the room again. Chloris was over in the dining room talking to Lester, smiling and gabbing away. She didn't know I was alive. Lucy was hanging around them trying to butt in once in a while. I knew she was wasting her time. When Chloris wants all the attention, she knows how to get it.

"Why do you want a picture of him, anyway?" Cindy was asking. "Don't you remember what he looked like?"

"That's the trouble," I said.

I tried to look sadder, in case she really had a picture of him hidden away some place. Then I added that I didn't remember him at all because I was so young when he left, and so forth. Cindy didn't cry. She looked across the room at Chloe.

"Your sister ought to remember," she said. "Won't she tell you?"

I hung my head. "I just wondered if you could . . . instead."

Cindy's lips twisted. "What exactly do you want to know?"

"What did he look like? Was he tall? Good-looking?"

She smiled at the way I blurted it out. "No, he wasn't tall," she said slowly, as if thinking back, trying to remember. "No, he was about average height, I'd say. Five eight or so. Stocky build. A little overweight, not too much. He had black hair and he was losing it fast. I remember that."

I couldn't imagine a grown man shooting himself because he was getting to be bald.

"How about good-looking?"

Cindy shrugged her shoulders and pulled at her lower lip with one hand to help her remember. "He wasn't any Adonis, but he wasn't bad-looking. He had nice eyes. Dark brown."

So little Jeff is like him, I thought, except for the teeth.

Cindy was looking at me as if she couldn't wait to get this thing over with. "What else do you want to know?"

For some reason, this was the most important one.

"Was he brave?"

She stood up straighter and looked puzzled. "What do you mean—brave?"

I waved my hands helplessly in a circle. "You know, Cindy. Brave."

She thought about it. Then her lip curled and she said sarcastically, "How brave do you have to be to be a patent attorney?"

I didn't want to ask her what that was and get another snotty answer. My eyes shifted again to Chloris and I wondered what made her so certain that Daddy was so brave. I couldn't remember anything. But I remembered Fidel and the rattlesnake. He hadn't hesitated a single second. And if that wasn't really brave, what was? Then I remembered suddenly why Chloris wasn't too impressed: she had fainted a second before he swung at the snake with his big axe.

I had a quick blinding thought. Had she fainted on purpose?

I'd never known her to faint before. If she were only pretending she would never have to admit how brave Fidel actually was. She could just look at you, smile and shrug, and say, "Sorry. I don't remember a thing about it. I fainted so I don't really know for sure whatever happened to that creepy snake."

On the ride back to our house, I didn't ask Cindy any more dumb questions. Chloris probably had some kind of slight crush on Lester. She kept talking to Cindy all the way home.

I didn't mind.

CHAPTER 14

MOM changed after Chloris and I blackballed
Fidel on the adoption. She wasn't as patient and
understanding about things with me as she had
been. I couldn't blame her exactly. I suppose she
had depended on me to be the good one, not to
string along with Chloris. I would have liked to
explain why I did it. The trouble was, I didn't
understand myself why I switched and voted
against him.

Fidel didn't act any different. He seemed to understand, even if I didn't. He must have known
Chloris had swung the whole deal, but he acted
toward her as if nothing had happened. Either
it was that warm Mexican blood in him, or he
just naturally had a good sugar-coated, sugar-lined
disposition. His laugh was just as hearty, his eyes
as friendly.

He was in his studio very early in the morning.
Painting his big wallsize canvasses, or fusing his
metals with the blowtorch, or hammering and
sawing away at his wooden sculptures. He worked
hard at it all day. After dinner, he would go back

again to work some more. He didn't know about holidays. The only times he took off from his work were when he was scrounging around for different materials, or when he had to take new things down to his gallery to sell.

He knocked off when Mom came home from work. He would mix her a tall Bloody Mary. Sometimes he would take her shoes off and rub her feet. Sometimes he made dinner for us—nothing fancy or even pretty to look at, stews mostly, a lot of beef or lamb mixed in a big kettle with potatoes and carrots and green peas and onions. He would make Mexican dishes, too. Tacos, tortillas, or fritos. The tacos were stuffed tortillas, with chicken or meat inside them.

Chloris accepted it all without batting an eye. "Big deal. I ate all this junk before we ever met him."

That was true and I couldn't argue. There are a lot of Mexican people in L.A. and the rest of us somehow got to dig the chili and the tortillas they sell at the drive-ins and supermarkets.

Fidel explained it all one evening. We had been talking about going downtown to Olvera Street. They have a square laid out there like a typical Mexican village, the shops with the Mexican and Indian things, the little cafes serving food. It's the Mexican quarter downtown. Their own ghetto. The blacks have one of their own, a little larger.

"All this land you are sitting on now," Fidel said, "was once owned by *Mexicanos*. From here to the sea. Up north past Malibu and Santa Barbara. Orange County, too—Yorba Linda, where our President was born—all California was *Mexicano*. They were the real Californios."

"How come?"

"They were the descendants of the early settlers. They inherited the land grants given by the Spanish and Mexican rulers."

"I mean, how come they got the land grants?" I said.

Fidel opened his brown eyes as if surprised. "You don't know? They don't teach you that in school history?"

"Maybe we haven't come to it yet," I said.

He looked at Chloris but she had her eyes down on the book in her lap. Then he told us about the original expedition in 1769. "The expedition of the Sword and the Cross. The Spanish *commandante* was Captain Jose Francisco Ortego. With him was Don Gaspar de Portola and Father Juniper Serra—have you never seen the California missions?"

I had to admit I hadn't.

Fidel laughed as if I had said something funny. "We will have to see them sometime. Father Serra spent his life building a chain of them across California."

Then he told how later the families connected with the original expedition were all given huge land grants by the Mexican rulers who replaced the Spanish. Thousands and thousands of acres. All the original California *ranchos*.

Chloris yawned and muttered something about going upstairs to finish her homework. Mom looked at her and nodded without saying anything. She already had been given Chloris's message—that she didn't think much of Fidel Mancha and she wouldn't give him the time of day.

"All the old *ranchos*," Fidel was saying. *"Boca de Santa Monica. Nuestra Senora del Refugio, Santiago de Santa Ana* and *San Julian.* Stretching all the way down the coast from Point Concepcion. And under the Treaty of *Guadalupe Hidalgo* in 1848, the United States agreed to recognize these land grants. Some descendants of the original settlers still live on these *ranchos.*"

Chloris yawned, stretched, and picking up her book started upstairs. She looked at me over her shoulder. "Coming?"

"In a minute. I want to hear the end."

She tossed her head and continued on up.

Fidel roared with laughter. He clapped his big hands.

"That's the whole story, little one. From now on, when you hear of some poor *chicano* complaining about how he is being treated, you will understand why. There was a time when he was somebody here in this country."

I stood facing him. "I don't have anything against the *chicanos,* Fidel. And remember, I didn't take their land away from them. I'm only eight years old."

Fidel's laughter followed me all the way upstairs.

Chloris was lying on her bed, waiting to look at me accusingly when I came in.

"Do you believe all that stuff?"

I nodded. "Didn't you?"

She looked pityingly at me. "Are you kidding? I'm not that stupid. He was making it all up."

"Gy. What for?"

"To impress us. To make us think he's somebody instead of a creepy Mexican."

"He *isn't* creepy."

She rolled over on her side facing away from me. "Prove it," she said.

I felt like socking her. It's too bad I didn't inherit a sweet disposition like Fidel Mancha's. Then I wouldn't get so mad.

CHAPTER 15

I DIDN'T realize how Chloris was goofing off at school until she brought home her next report card. She had poor marks in almost every subject. She threw it down on Mom's writing desk and acted pretty cool about it, but I could tell she didn't feel so cool inside.

When Mom came home and read it, she nearly flipped. She stormed up to Chloris's room and didn't bother knocking on the closed door.

"What kind of a report card do you call this?"

I could hear it all from inside my room. I could have heard it from the top of the mountain behind the house.

"So what?" Chloris said.

Smack, I heard.

"That's for being insolent," Mom said. "From now on, you will do an hour's extra studying every night and . . ."

"Every night?" yelled Chloris. "I won't . . . I . . ."

Smack. Another good one from Mom.

She went on as if nothing had happened to interrupt her chain of thought. "You will do an hour's study every night. There will be no TV until your homework is done. You will do better on your next report card, or your TV and other privileges will be taken away. Is that understood?"

Chloris mumbled something.

I didn't hear any other smack so I figured she had made the right mumble. Mom started to walk out and Chloris said something else. I couldn't hear it clearly but Mom must have because she started to walk back.

"What was that you said about a creepy Mexican?"

"Well, he is," Chloris yelled. "It's not my fault and I don't know why you had to marry him and . . ."

This was the best *smack* of all. It was followed by several minor ones.

"Fidel is my husband," Mom said. "You will treat him with respect. Do you understand?"

Silence.

Smack. Mom wasn't tired at all from doing a good hard day's work down at Bontel's.

"Okay, okay." Chloris was crying. "Leave me alone."

"With pleasure," Mom said. She went out without closing the door. She started down the steps. I heard the door slam—Mom's arms weren't that long—and her start back up. She opened the door again and there was another *smack*.

"And don't ever slam your door on me again," Mom said as she went out, slamming the door herself.

Chloris cried for about an hour. When it was time for dinner, Mom asked me to call her. Chloris said from behind her door that she didn't want any. I went down alone. When Chloris is crying, she doesn't want anybody to be in there with her. Fidel glanced at her empty place as Mom started to serve dinner.

"Trouble?" he asked.

"A little."

He sighed. "It was bound to happen."

For once, he wasn't too cheerful at the table. He lit his pipe and finished his coffee.

"Can I do anything?" he asked.

Mom said she didn't think so.

Fidel sighed again and looked at me. "How are things with you?"

"Fine," I said.

"No problems?"

"No."

"Good," he said. Then he stretched and excused himself and went back to his studio.

I was finishing my ice cream when I heard a strange sound. I looked up. Mom was crying. *Gy,* I thought, *I haven't seen her do that since . . . since . . . since a long time ago.*

I didn't let myself get away with it. *Since she was married to Daddy,* I told myself. *I remember!*

That night was when the cold war started in Fidel's house in Tigertail Canyon. Chloris who had never acted even half-friendly toward Fidel turned him off completely now. It made Mom uptight and angry. I didn't go along with Chloris because I liked Fidel.

"Whose side are you on," she asked me.

"Nobody's."

"The way you suck up to him and hang around him, somebody would think he was your own father."

"Well, I like him," I said. "Besides he's Mom's husband. And I got to show respect for him."

Chloris jeered. "You're too much."

"He can be a nice father," I said. "What's wrong with that?"

She became very pale. Her hazel eyes glowed and she leaned toward me, almost rigid. "Because he's not," she said in a low tight voice. "He's not our father, he was never intended to be our father, and he's not going to be our father. Not ever! You got that, you creep? Never!"

By this time, she was practically screaming, and I started to move away. She reached out and caught my arm and squeezed it hard. "You better not let me catch you sucking up to him again."

I struggled to get out of her grip but she was stronger. "Or what?" I asked.

"Or I'll never talk to you again," she said. She released her hold and walked away without once looking back.

I was still outside the house rubbing my arm when Fidel's studio door opened. He came out stretching, taking huge gulps of the evening air before he turned and saw me holding my arm.

"Is something the matter?"

I dropped my hand. "Oh, no. Nothing."

"The way you were rubbing your arm, I thought you were hurt."

"Oh, no. I wasn't rubbing. Scratching. I was scratching it. I guess some bug bit me."

He stepped closer. "I'd better have a look."

"No, it's okay," I said nervously, starting to back away. He stopped, looking puzzled, his head tilted back. "It's okay," I said again. "Honest."

I waved to him, backed off a few more steps, then turned and ran. I ran completely around the house to the side facing the road. I remembered the hurt puzzled look in his eyes as I backed away, and felt awful.

I had a hard time falling asleep that night. I knew Chloris would keep her word and cut me out of her life if I disobeyed her. That meant being mean to Fidel. I didn't want to think of what it meant to Mom. I wondered why I still liked Chloris despite the way she twisted things around to suit her purpose.

It's because you are sisters, I told myself. *You have this bond between you.*

Then I felt myself drifting away and dreaming. I saw Daddy. He smiled at me and stretched out his arms. I started to run to him. Then I stopped, frightened. He didn't have any teeth.

I ran away screaming. He laughed shrilly, a toothless laugh, and I kept running until I couldn't hear him any more.

CHAPTER 16

IF ALL the early *Mexicanos* given the land grants in California were like Fidel, I could see how they lost it all. He was so good-natured he would have given it away.

Here was Chloris going out of her way to be insulting and mean to him, and what did he do? He laughed. If she snubbed him and walked past without even saying hello, he didn't appear to take notice. Instead, he rewarded her.

One day he brought her a picture he had painted. It was small and very pretty, a purple flower so perfect you could almost smell it or expect the petals to fall off in your hand. Chloris didn't smile or thank him. She took it upstairs and threw it under the bed, muttering.

"Who needs his creepy flowers."

She had always wanted a guitar. Mom kept stalling her off, telling her the usual, "Some day, some day," hoping, I guess, that it would be like a lot of other things Chloris thought she wanted and later didn't. Fidel must have heard her going on about this guitar she had to have. He walked in one day carrying a big black odd-shaped case, put it down at Chloris' feet and smiled.

"I hope it is a good one," he said, turned and went out.

Chloris looked blankly at me. "What's the matter with him?" she said crossly.

I pointed to the big black case. "What is it?"

With her lips twisted in distaste, her face flushed, she bent down and opened the metal snaps.

I gaped. "A guitar!"

Chloris looked angrily at me. "Well, what did you think it was, dumbbell—a saxophone?"

"A guitar! Just what you always wanted."

"Only not from him," she said, staring down at its gleaming golden surface.

I picked it up by the neck. "Here. Aren't you going to play it?" She didn't say anything, just kept looking at it, sort of stunned. I lifted it out of its case and put it on her lap. "Go on. Try playing it."

She shook her head. "Not now."

"How come?"

Her eyes blazed. "If you don't mind, it's my guitar, and it's up to me to decide."

I didn't get it. "Gy!"

She set it back carefully in its case, closed it, then carried it toward the stairs. "I'm going to my room. I don't want any company."

"Gy!" I felt like kicking her.

I heard her door close. I listened intently and heard a few strumming sounds. She started to hum a song and then stopped. For a few seconds I couldn't hear anything, then her window scraped open. I figured she was getting ready to show off to the neighbors how she could play a guitar. Instead, I heard this awful crash.

I ran upstairs. "What happened?"

She was leaning out the open window, looking down. She stepped back as I came rushing over to look. My jaw dropped about a yard.

The guitar lay on some of the rocks below in the flower garden. It was broken into a lot of jagged pieces. "Gy!" I cried. "What happened!"

Chloris looked blankly at me and shrugged. "It dropped," she said, and walked out of the room humming.

Fidel didn't say anything but the next morning the pieces were gone. He probably didn't even say anything to Mom or I guess she would have let Chloris have it again. I was becoming very angry with Fidel. Why didn't he pick her up and shake her and scare her into some sense? I sure didn't go along with all this laughing business.

He bought her a bicycle. It had eleven gears and the kind of high looping handlebars she liked. She left it out on the road. A truck ran over it.

A tennis racket came next, with a sealed can of new balls. The racket was one of those Billy Jean King models and had that real great tennis racket look to it. Chloris had some pictures of Billy Jean in her room. She had told me that some day she would be a Wimbledon champ, too. You wouldn't believe where that tennis racket wound up. High up on a tree. Almost out of sight.

Chloris sighed. "It slipped."

I reminded her how quickly she had totalled her bike, also. Chloris said, "Those truck drivers never look where they're driving."

The next day I looked for the yellow-framed tennis racket high on that tree branch, and it was gone. I figured some bird had managed to bring it home to his family, saying, "Hey look what I found. Can't we use some of this stuff?"

"You can't keep doing this to Fidel," I told Chloris. "I don't care if you never talk to me again. From now on I'm going to be nice to him."

She shrugged. "Go ahead. Be a creep if you want to."

I took the first opportunity to tell Fidel how I felt about it all. "I don't think she really means what she's doing," I told him. "She never used to be this way."

Fidel patted my head, smiling. "She has her problems, that one."

"Maybe you ought to stop wasting your money. I don't think she's going to like anything you bring her."

Fidel puckered his lips, his brown eyes thoughtful. "Perhaps you're right, little one. But it is something we have to work out. Some things are more difficult than others."

I shook my head. He didn't know Chloris at all. "It's not going to work. She won't take anything from you. I know her."

He patted my head again, gently. "Some women are hard to please. Wouldn't you agree?"

I couldn't. I couldn't see Fidel calling Chloris a woman, for one thing. "You're only wasting all your good money," I told him.

Fidel laughed. "Money! What is it? It is not nearly so important as people think."

"Gy, if money isn't important, what is?"

"Here." He was patting his broad chest. "Inside here. How a person thinks is important. But how one feels, that is the most important of all."

I looked up at Fidel, kind of disgusted. Had he had all those hundred thousand acres given to the original Don Bernardo Yorba during the Mexican reign, he would have given them all away if he felt like it.

A few days later, a big white box was delivered to our house. The label said Bloomington's Department Store, and it was addressed to Chloris Carpenter, Ms. She finally showed some excitement.

"It's from Grandma Helen!" she cried. She tore the colored tape off the box and lifted the lid. Underneath a lot of white tissue paper was a purple polka-dotted Granny dress with a white ruffled collar.

Chloris screamed with delight. "Just what I wanted."

She grabbed it out of the box, pressed it to her throat and ran across the room to her full-length mirror where she swayed from side to side, making happy new-dress sounds, admiring the way the dress touched her toes.

"Bloomington's Store isn't in Cleveland," I said. "It says right here on the label—Beverly Hills."

Chloris stopped swaying and frowned. "What?"

I reached down into the box for a small card in a little white envelope. "Here's the card that goes with it."

"What does it say?" she asked, half-smiling.

I read it out loud. "Love, from Fidel."

She snatched the dress away from her throat, her face red and angry. "Why, the rotten creep! The sneaky rotten creep!"

"It looks great on you," I said. "Aren't you going to wear it?"

"That'll be the day!" she said. She rolled the dress into a ball and threw it on the floor of her closet. "I'm not wearing his creepy dress," she panted.

"You're acting real crazy," I said. "It's a beautiful dress. It will look great on you."

Chloris tossed her head. "Not if it's from him, it won't."

I couldn't take my eyes off that sad-looking dress on the floor of her closet. "Maybe you ought to hang it up. In case some day you change your mind."

She turned and walked stiffly across the room. She picked the dress up and held it out by the tips of her fingers. She walked over and stood in front of me holding it out like that. "Here," she said. "You want it? It's all yours."

I took a step back. "No, thanks. It's your present."

"Well, I didn't ask him for it. I don't want it. I don't want anything from him."

"You're making a terrible mistake," I said. "Fidel is a real nice person. I bet you your own Daddy wouldn't have bought you a beautiful dress like that!"

Her mouth opened. I watched fascinated as no sound came out. Her face paled and I saw tears forming in her eyes. Then her arm came up and I ducked.

The ball of purple polka-dotted Granny dress sailed over my head.

CHAPTER 17

Mom didn't forget the study period for Chloris. After dinner, when the table had been cleared and we were finished helping Mom with the dishes, Chloris had to break out her school books. She used the dining room table which was big enough for a ping-pong game. Mom would go inside the den and watch TV. On warm nights Fidel forgot about his studio work and joined her, to sit close on the couch, and sometimes hold hands.

My marks weren't so hot in school but they weren't the worst, either. Anyway, Mom thought it wouldn't hurt if I tried a little harder to put some brains in my head. I sat at the opposite end of the table from Chloris. The big rule was we were there to study, not talk.

It took Chloris a long time to settle down. She had to go through a lot of different sitting positions to get comfortable. That took ten to fifteen minutes. When she finally was set, she had to go to the bathroom. When she came back, she spent another ten to fifteen minutes flipping the pages of her books. I could see her heart wasn't in it.

After a few nights of this Mom caught on and laid down the law again. Chloris complained about this or that. She was tired. Her eyes hurt. She got leg cramps from that creepy chair of Fidel's. The table was too high. The light was awful. Nobody else in her class had to do this. Her marks were good enough for the teacher. What good would it do?

Mom listened. She let Chloris run on and on with this excuse or that until she finally ran out of ideas. Mom asked her then if she was done. Chloris had her head propped on her hand, and admitted she was.

"If I recall correctly," Mom said in a strangely quiet way, "and I'm sure I do, your dear father whom you love so dearly was pretty strict about your marks in school. Do you remember the many spankings he gave you for bringing home bad report cards?"

Chloris forgot how tired she was. Her eyes grew hot with anger. "That's not true. He never."

Mom didn't bat an eye. "Just think about it. It's all there in your memory. And if you've forgotten about it, I haven't."

"He never. He never," Chloris yelled. "He never touched me, he never hit me. He didn't care what kind of marks I got."

Mom looked down at her steadily. "You're sure about that, too, I suppose?"

Chloris fidgeted and got very red-faced. "Well,

okay, maybe he wanted me to get good marks. But he never hit me. He was never mean to me the way you are!"

Mom's lips trembled and her voice became a little rocky. "I'm sorry you feel that way. If you don't choose to remember, I can't help you. But regardless, you are going to study for at least an hour every night until your marks improve."

"Weekends, too?" howled Chloris.

"No," Mom said. "Not yet, anyhow. If you study, and your marks and schoolwork get better, that won't be necessary. But if they don't you'll have that to look forward to, I'm afraid."

With that she walked away. Chloris slid her eyes to me but I was too smart to get caught. Mine stayed fixed on the same page I'd been looking at since the argument began. She reached out and grabbed the top book off the pile in the center and yanked it open.

"This is a creepy subject," she said. "I always hated it."

"That's mine," I said.

She glared at me. "What?"

"You took my *New Math* book. Yours is the other pile."

"Thanks a lot for telling me!"

"You're welcome," I said.

"What's a patent attorney?"

Mom put her hand to her head and pushed back some hair. "What is this—a conspiracy?"

"No, honest. Cindy told me at the party for Jeff that Daddy was a patent attorney."

Mom was puzzled. "What made her say that?"

"Isn't it true?"

"Certainly, it's true. Your father was a patent attorney. But I don't see . . ."

"I happened to ask her what he did to make money."

"What made you ask Cindy that?"

"I don't remember. So, anyway, what's a patent attorney?"

"A patent attorney is a lawyer who takes care of patents for inventors."

"Oh," I said.

"Aren't you going to ask me now what a patent is?"

"Okay. Yeah. What's that?"

"It's a legal safeguard to protect the inventor to keep another person from taking his idea and using it for profit."

"That's what Daddy did in his office?"

"Yes," Mom said crisply. "Among other things."

Chloris was on her bed listening to the Stones.

"Did you know Daddy was a patent attorney?"

"Of course. Who didn't know that?"

"Do you know what one is?"

She blinked. "Of course. They sell things for those people."

"Right on," I said.

Grandma Grace, Mom's mother, came to our house in Tigertail to see how the natives lived. I asked her what took her so long.

"I don't trust newlyweds," she said.

"How come?"

"Let's skip that, and you can show me around."

She liked everything, she said even if it wasn't her cup of tea. Fidel was very good with her and let her walk all around his studio. He even let her touch things."

"My," Grandma Grace said. "Why does everything have to be so big?"

"There are some near-sighted buyers," Fidel said. "I don't want them to miss anything."

Grandma Grace found herself looking at the big hobby horse. "My," she said. "That's very clever. How much are you asking for that?"

Fidel shook his head. "It is not for sale."

"Oh? Why not?"

Fidel said it just wasn't.

"Well, why not?"

Grandma Grace used *why not* almost as much as I used *how come?*

"I like it," Fidel said. He wagged his thumb at me. "This one likes it."

"But you probably could make a lot of money," Grandma Grace said. "It's very clever and unusual. I've never seen anything like it."

"Let me show you something else," he said.

"It's all right," she said. "I'm just looking, not buying."

I took her on a tour of the house. She complained a lot about all those steps and different landings. "How do you keep from getting lost here?" she said. She liked my room and the one Chloris had. She looked out my window toward the mountain. "What's up there?" she asked.

"Snakes."

Grandma Grace turned away quickly. "Goodness!"

Fidel prepared a special outdoor barbecue for her. There were hamburgers for Chloris and me, because that's what we wanted, and a lot of meat and onions and green peppers stuck on some skinny swords for them. Grandma Grace drank a lot of wine, more than was good for her, she said. And as dusk deepened into twilight and the hills behind changed from green to purple and then to a velvety blackness, she sighed.

"It's certainly very quiet here. What do you people do for excitement?"

Then the crickets got to work and woke up the night birds. The birds started asking everybody around what time it was and where was everybody and how were things, and that woke up the dogs. In a little while, Grandma Grace had had it.

"What's on TV tonight?" she asked.

CHAPTER 18

EXCEPT for carrying her there after killing the snake, Fidel had never been inside Chloris' room since she moved into his house with the rest of us. She had a big colored sign outside the door, which was always closed, on which she had printed:

KEEP OUT • NO ADMITENCE

He visited with me once in a while. Sometimes to tuck me in. Sometimes to do something to keep the bureau from wobbling. He made me a big basket out of stiff cardboard so I could practice shooting with my soft ball in case the Lakers ever decided to let girls on their team. This time he barely stepped inside my room. He beckoned me to him.

"How do you feel about your father?"

That was a tougher question to answer than I thought.

"Gy," I said after about a million years, "I don't know. I don't remember much about him. I was very little."

"I know," he said. "Would you like to visit his grave? Put some flowers around it, in his memory?"

That seemed a nice idea. "Okay. Sure."

"Would you ask your sister to come out, please?"

I did as he asked. I knocked twice and Chloris asked me who it was. That was a dumb question because our signal is two knocks, whether it's for her door or my door. I told her it was me and she asked what I wanted and I told her. Come out.

"Why?"

"Because," I answered.

"I'm too busy," she said.

I could hear her phonograph going so I knocked two more times. She came to the door and opened it a big half inch.

"What do you want?"

I backed off. "Come out."

She looked at me, shrugged and came out. "What is it?"

I pointed over my shoulder. "Fidel wants to talk to you."

She saw him instantly and couldn't get out of it. She gave him her TV star look. *Do you want to talk to me?*

"Would you like to visit your father's grave?" Fidel asked.

On a bright Saturday we all piled into Fidel's big ranch wagon. I know it's a station wagon but that's what the thing on it says. *Ranchwagon.* He used it to bring his lumber and junk back and forth in. This time he had put back the seats and cleaned it so it looked really nice. Fidel looked nice, too. He was wearing a white shirt and a tie and a coat that matched his pants. I had never seen him with a tie before. I wondered if that was the rule at cemeteries.

Along the way he stopped at a florist shop. He got out of the car. "Come girls, and pick out your flowers."

We swivelled our heads from him to Mom. "Just do as he says. He's doing this for you."

Chloris shrugged and joined me following after Fidel. He let his hand sweep along the various pots of flowers lining the red brick floor of the florist. "Pick what you want."

I looked at him. "What's it for?"

"In honor of your father. To decorate his grave."

"I could have told you that," Chloris said.

Mom waited in the station wagon until we came back, each with an armful. She didn't try to smell them, or smile and say my, how beautiful they were. She merely nodded, looked at her wristwatch and said we'd better be going, if we were going.

Westlawn Hills looked like a very nice cemetery. There were neat lawns and shade trees and all the cars driving around drove slowly. Nobody was cutting anybody off, or yelling "Stupid Jerk, watch where you're goin'" or playing their radios loud. It really looked like another world. It was too bad all the dead people didn't get a chance to see how nice and peaceful it was, and all the respect everybody was showing for all the dead, even those they didn't know. Fidel stopped at a little brick house near the entrance and went inside.

"Where's he going?" I asked Mom. She told me, to get directions to the plot. I asked what that was. Mom told me that's where Daddy was.

Fidel came out in a few minutes and looked at us before getting back into his car. "Well, you are all looking very pretty," he said.

I think we were, too. Chloris and I had new dresses that Grandma Grace bought for us. Grandma Helen in Cleveland had sent us the money for shoes and they were nice and shining. Fidel had bought us the flowers. I had a lot of pink and white ones. Chloris had picked a lot of purple and red ones. Mom was dressed up nice, too, wearing her dark blue shift with the belt and brass buttons. I supposed she used her own working money for that, unless Fidel gave her some.

Fidel drove slowly around one curve and up another. There were rows of stones covering the sloping green grass on each side of us. Some of the stones were very large, some small, and some you could barely see.

"What are all those stones for?"

"Those are tombstones, dumbbell."

Fidel glanced at a little slip of paper in his hand and stopped. "We walk from here. Come on, girls."

He got out, opened the door, and Chloris and I got out. Chloris looked at Mom. "Aren't you coming?"

Mom shook her head, her lips tight, her face

pale. "This is for you girls. You go on with Fidel. He'll show you the grave."

Fidel looked up from his slip of paper. "C 53," he said. He started off walking slowly, looking from one stone to another.

"How can we find it?" I asked. There were too many stones.

Fidel explained how the plots were laid out according to the alphabet and numbers. He showed me we were between Row C and Row D, and all we had to do was follow the numbers up until we came to 53. Chloris ran ahead without waiting for me.

"I found it, I found it!" she cried.

She was standing looking down at something. It wasn't even a stone, just some words marked on a framed plate in the ground.

"Is that where he is?" I whispered.

Fidel nodded, pointing to the marker at my feet. I read what it said slowly. I hadn't ever known my own father's name.

LAWRENCE CARPENTER
1932—1969

All the letters and numbers were metal and looked as if they had been carved out of something. I looked at Chloris. Her face was very red and she was crying. I looked at Fidel. He stood aside very quietly, his face without any expression. I didn't know what to do. I didn't actually feel like crying. I tugged at Fidel's sleeve.

"What do we do?" I whispered into his ear when he leaned down.

"You place your flowers around," he said. His hand went out in a sweeping gesture to indicate the area for the flowers.

Before I could move, Chloris had dumped all her flowers down. "This is for you, Daddy dear," she said. I couldn't remember ever seeing her look so sweet and angelic. I saw she had picked the best spot, right near the marker. "Any place around the grave is good," Fidel said softly.

I placed mine down at the opposite side, spreading them out so they would look like more flowers. Chloris was doing the same with hers, moving them around, fussing with them, trying one combination of reds and purples and then another.

"It's from me, Daddy dear. From Chloris," she said, crying. "Your own little girl."

I knew I was his own little girl, too, but I still didn't feel like crying. I looked around. There were other people around different stones. Some of them were just standing looking at the stones. Others were placing their flowers. Several of them were praying and crying.

Before I knew it I was crying, too.

Fidel handed me his big white handkerchief and helped me blow my nose. The people at the other grave had stopped crying now and were walking away slowly. I had finished my crying now and I looked at Chloris. She was still going strong.

Suddenly she threw herself on the ground, her arms flung out as if she were hugging the grave.

"Take me with you, Daddy," she said. "I want to be with you."

I couldn't stand it. I looked up at Fidel and he continued looking down as quietly as a TV Indian. He let her cry and cry until her body stopped twitching and jerking, then he leaned over and touched her arm.

"It is all right now. Your father has heard your prayer. You can get up now."

She turned her face up. It was tear-stained and dirty. She let Fidel help her up but shook her head when he offered his handkerchief. She stared down at the marker, her head cocked. Suddenly she lifted her hand, pointing to the inscription.

"Just look how young he was. 1932 to 1969. Only thirty-five."

When we got back to the car, Mom was still inside.

"Are you all right?" Fidel asked.

"Yes." She looked at Chloris and me. "Are you finished or do you want to stay longer?"

I couldn't see any reason for staying. It was becoming too sad. Chloris hesitated, then shrugged, and opened the car door. She went inside, and I followed. Mom sat up front with Fidel. I saw him touch her hand as he put the key in the ignition.

"Everything is all right," he told her.

Mom looked relieved when he started the car up and we moved slowly around the first curve. I could understand her not caring about jumping out and decorating her husband's grave since he had left her for other women. I hadn't seen any flowers from Cindy there, either, and I realized Daddy had left her, too, after they got married, even before his new son was born. I felt a little sad about him dying so young, but even without *New Math* I knew he was more than thirty-five when he did it. And his name was supposed to be Larry Carpenter, not Lawrence.

CHAPTER 19

GRANDMA Grace was on the phone. "Well, how are you today, pumpkin?"

"I'm still feeling kind of sad. Chloris and I brought flowers to Daddy's grave."

"Yes, so I heard. Well, you did it and now there's nothing to be sad about."

"I guess. What happens to people when they die, Grandma?"

"How would I know?" she said sharply. "Besides, don't talk to me about dying. I've enough trouble living." I wasn't always sure when Grandma Grace was joking. "Let me talk to your mother."

I got Mom and she spoke with Grandma. I was still in the room when I heard her say. "No. I don't know what's wrong with her. She's been relating to him more and more lately. It's become an obsession. She's fantasizing him and his life. She talks now about dying so she could be with him."

I knew they weren't talking about me.

"No," Mom continued, "she still hasn't accepted Fidel as my husband. She slights and rebuffs him, yet he still treats her with the utmost kindness. He's been marvelous."

Grandma had an opinion on that, then it was Mom's turn again. "I've an appointment this week with a therapist. Dr. Smythe. Supposed to be excellent with children. No, I haven't told Chloris yet. Probably this evening."

I went outside. Fidel was away picking up more lumber. His *Ranchwagon* would be filled when he came back with those big beams he liked. I heard a noise inside his studio and stopped, curious. Then footfalls. His door opened slowly and, to my amazement, it was Chloris backing out slowly, carefully. I ducked behind a shrub near the big shade tree. She waited a moment to be sure nobody was watching, then quickly pulled his door shut behind her, and ran around the house. For an instant, her face had been lit by a sly strange expression.

What was up? I wondered. Since that earlier visit with me to look at Fidel's big toy horse Chloris had never stepped foot inside his studio. I thought about that weird look on her face, almost a smile of triumph. I waited a few seconds, then carefully opened the studio door and went in.

I looked around carefully. Had she played any mean trick on Fidel? Everything seemed in its usual messy state, his paintings and statues all standing there, his blowtorch off. I was determined to find out if she had done something wrong. I didn't hear the *Ranchwagon* until it stopped in the driveway.

He came in lugging a beam nearly as big as he was. He pulled it across the room, propped it up against the wall, and then saw me. His eyes flicked sideways for a moment, just long enough for me to notice.

"Hi, sweetheart, what are you doing—taking a secret ride on the big horse?"

I lied, gratefully. "Yes. I hope you don't mind, Fidel."

He laughed. "What for? It's for you. I'm too old to play on a horse." I started to edge away. "You don't have to leave. You can play some more, if you want."

"No, thanks. It's okay."

I went out quickly, noticing that once more I had managed to leave a curious puzzled expression in Fidel's eyes.

In my dream later that night I was watching a fire. The flames leaped higher and higher. The whole canyon was on fire. People were screaming, running off like crazy. The animals ran right along with them. A deer jumped out of Fidel's window, smiling as if it did that all the time. I smelled the smoke. I heard a shout. Fidel was chasing the deer, shaking his fist angrily. That's funny, I thought, usually he's so goodnatured about things. The smoke got thicker, swirling around me and I started to cough.

I coughed some more and started to shake. Big hands were pulling at me. I opened my eyes and there was Fidel.

"All right, little one," he said softly. "Do not be afraid. Come. We are going outside for a little bit."

Before I could say *How come?* I was in his arms, held tight as he ran down the steps. I saw Mom coming out of Chloris' room leading her by the hand. Chloris was rubbing her eyes and complaining she wanted to sleep. There were a few people standing around outside and Fidel handed me to one of them. He rushed back to Mom and Chloris as they came to the doorway and picked them both up at the same time, trundling them a few yards past me before setting them down.

Then he was running toward his studio where flames licked inside the window. Smoke leaked through the wood, the air around filled with it, and I realized suddenly why I had been coughing. There was a shattering crash and I saw Fidel smash the window with a board. In the distance I heard sirens wailing.

We were on fire.

Men brought hoses and the water hissed as the fire fought back. Fidel kept bringing things out of his studio, throwing them on the ground and men with the hoses soaked them with water. In a little while it was all over. The water won.

Neighbors loaned us coats to shiver in. Nobody thought of shoes or slippers and my feet were freezing on the cold grass. A police car came up, its radio blaring calls. The fire truck had its own radio going, too. Mostly the firemen and the police seemed to be trading addresses, one after the other, while red lights flashed.

I grabbed Mom. "What happened?"

She looked tense and worried. "I don't know. Fidel's studio caught on fire somehow. He got me up in time to rouse Chloris while he carried you out."

"But how did it happen?"

"Nobody knows."

The firemen checked our house thoroughly. They looked into all the corners with flashlights, checked the wiring, even climbed the roof and checked the dormers before permitting us to go back inside. Though nothing in Fidel's house had been burned the smell was awful.

He came in later, looking tired, smeared with soot and dirt, his shirt soaked with water, his shoes squishing when he walked.

"Is everything ruined?" Mom asked gently. "All your work?"

"Not everything," he said gruffly. He shook his big head and the water sprayed off in droplets. "It could have been worse."

"How come?"

He looked at me. "The entire house could have caught the flame. Then the canyon. The entire ridge. All the houses. All the people and the animals. They would all be running like crazy trying to get away from the forest fire."

"It's my dream," I shrieked. "It's my dream!"

Fidel and Mom looked at me carefully.

"I dreamed it all," I explained. "Tonight. I saw it all happening just like you said, Fidel. The whole canyon on fire. The people and animals running like crazy. I even smelled the smoke it was so real. That's when you broke the dream by waking me."

He looked at Mom. "Does she have premonitions often?"

Mom shook her head. "I think it's by association. She probably smelled the smoke in her sleep and instantly dreamed the fire."

He shrugged, his shoulders sagging. "Yes, I suppose."

I went after him as he started out again. "But what really happened? How could a fire start in your studio? Were you working with your blowtorch?"

"No. I was sleeping not working. But I think somebody else was using my blowtorch."

"What do you mean?"

"The turpentine I use in my paint had been spilled over the floor and over my statues. Then, whoever did that flicked the blowtorch on. That was all it needed. It was a senseless thing for a person to do. It could have been very dangerous. We all could have died in the fire."

I stamped my foot hard. "Who could have done a dumb thing like that?"

Fidel tapped his temple. "Anybody who is not sound here."

I agreed. A person would have to be crazy to do that.

"Also there are people who start fires for their own reasons."

"Like what?" I asked him.

"Sometimes it makes them feel important. They have frightened a lot of people. Done a lot of damage. They can look around and say to themselves, 'I did all that!'"

That sounded pretty crazy to me, too.

"Some people start fires because they feel they have been neglected. They want more attention paid to them."

"Gy," I said. "But who would do a thing like that to you?"

His eyes looked deeply into mine. Then he smiled sadly and patted my head. "I don't know, sweetheart. The only one who knows for sure is the one who did it."

My heart thumped as my mind suddenly skipped back to that afternoon when Fidel looked at me with surprise as he brought his big planks inside the studio. It was the first time I had gone in when he wasn't there. The door was never locked but I had never gone in before. I realized he didn't know that. I shivered suddenly. Did what he had said apply to me? Was I supposed to feel neglected?

Chloris was leaning toward me, smiling slyly. "What were you doing in there anyway today?"

Without looking, I knew Fidel and Mom were staring at me. Chloris couldn't have meant to make it appear I had something to do with the fire. I heard her voice again, soft and wrapped up in a sly smile.

"Well, can't you think of a good excuse?"

I shook my head. Words flooded my brain but by the time they reached my mouth they felt all mixed up.

My own sister Chloris.

The biggest creep of all!

"I didn't," I started to say. "I couldn't . . . I only went in because . . ."

"Because," she repeated, smiling.

All I had to do now was say I'd gone in because I thought *she* had done something. But I couldn't say it.

I started to cry instead.

CHAPTER 20

CHLORIS came back from her first visit to Dr. Smythe so upset and mad I forgot I wasn't going to speak to her any more. I listened to her throw her things around the room and crying until I couldn't stand it. Because she was such a rat fink about the fire, I didn't even bother to knock twice on her door.

"What happened?" I said.

She turned on me angrily. "I didn't send for you. Go away."

I pretended my hearing was bad. "Did you go to the therapist?"

"She's no therapist," Chloris yelled. "She's a creep."

I sat down on her bed. "How come?"

Chloris finished kicking her favorite green pillow around the room. "Are you still here? Visiting hours are over. Go away."

"Beverly Brandon's brother Mark went to a therapist for two whole years." I said.

Chloris stared. "You're kidding. Mark?"

"That's what she told me. He liked it. He told

her he finally found somebody who understood his problem.":

I knew Chloris was still hoping Mark Brandon would ask her out on a date sometimes when she got a little older. She flopped down beside me. "What problem?"

"I don't know. I think they're supposed to be secret problems. Nobody is allowed to discuss them."

"No kidding?" Chloris said. "Well, my problem isn't any secret. I don't care who knows about it."

"You're right. It's your problem so you should be allowed to talk about it all you want."

She squinted thoughtfully. "You think so, Jen?"

"Right on, babe." I kind of wished she would get to it soon so I'd know what it was all about.

"Well, you know," she said, hesitantly, "it's me and Daddy. You know. Our relationship."

"Sure."

"You know how much I love him, don't you?"

"You bet," I said. I wondered if it was worth one more *right on* but decided to hold off.

"Well, according to this creepy Dr. Smythe, she thinks that maybe I'm overdoing it. Can you imagine?"

I put on my amazed look. "No kidding?"

"I'm not kidding. She spent about an hour trying to tell me that was over and done with. That I was a little girl then but that now my Daddy is dead and I have to go on and grow up. Can you imagine?"

I shook my head. "She sure sounds like some creep. Gy!"

Chloris was so happy, she nearly hugged me. "Exactly. Then she gave me a lot of jazz about having to know myself, who I was and what I stood for, and like that."

"You mean, she doesn't think you know who you are?"

"Well, not exactly. She thinks I think I'm who I am, only that's not what she means. She means who am I, Chloris Carpenter, in the world."

"Oh," I said. "What did you tell her?"

"I said I would keep on loving my Daddy no matter who I was and how old I got to be when I grew up."

"What did she say to that?"

" 'Come back next week.' "

Grandma Grace called Mom again to find out how things were going.

"Awful. Simply awful. I think I'm going to lose my mind."

I wished I'd heard how Grandma Grace handled that.

"You wouldn't believe the garbage that child has in her mind," Mom went on. "All from the lies fed her by my darling mother-in-law. Would you believe it if I told you that child actually believes I'm responsible for her father's suicide?" Mom waited a while. "I asked you a question, Mother. I'd appreciate an answer."

I liked the way they went at it. That real mother and daughter stuff, right on!

"No," Mom was saying. "I will not get angry if you tell me the truth. What is this truth you want to tell me? No, mother, honest, I won't get angry. What? No, I won't get upset, either. Go on, I'm listening."

She listened for several foot taps then, when she was about to answer, Grandma Grace speeded up her end of it, and Mom had to grimace and swing her leg and make a lot of doodles all over her telephone pad. "No, I am not angry," she said loudly. "Go on, please." After a while, she said, "Are you quite finished? You're certain you didn't leave anything out? Well, thanks a lot for the information. I don't know what I'd do without your help."

She hung the phone back on. She looked so mad I decided it was safe to take a chance.

"What did Grandma Grace say?"

"She said she told me never to marry your father in the first place," Mom snapped.

Later, Mom and Fidel discussed Chloris' attitude.

"It's nothing to be so concerned about," Fidel said. "She will come out of it when she is ready."

"When she's ready?" Mom explained. "Who can wait that long? She might take forever!"

Fidel laughed. "She has everybody fooled. She is just playing her own part in her own game.

When she gets tired of it, she will be all right."

"Wonderful," Mom said. "Since when did you become a child psychiatrist?"

Fidel shrugged. "I may not be very good but I work cheap."

Mom laughed.

Two more visits to Dr. Smythe in Beverly Hills didn't help Chloris much, according to Mom. Grandma Grace was visiting us and they were having tea. I was supposed to be doing something to occupy myself.

"She was worse this week, if that's possible. She told Dr. Smythe I drove him into the arms of other women because I was so wrapped up in myself."

"Well," Grandma Grace said. "That's a slight exaggeration perhaps but I've always felt that . . . ."

"Oh, Mother, will you cut that out?"

"I was only trying to help," Grandma said. "Are there any more cookies?"

"If you ate less cookies and listened to what I was telling you, perhaps we could figure out something."

"I knew you didn't want my help," Grandma said.

"All right, Mother. What do *you* think we should do now?"

"I don't know," Grandma said. "She's a difficult girl. Of course, you were no bargain either when you were her age."

"I suppose I wasn't. But I didn't live in a fantasy world. I accepted reality. Didn't I?"

"You never accepted washing dishes," Grandma Grace said. "You were always afraid to get your fingers wet."

"I was? Why?"

"I don't know. I think you were afraid your fingers were going to fall off if they got too wet."

After her third visit, Chloris stuck two extra KEEP OUT THIS MEENS YOU signs on her door. I knocked twice and she said, okay come in.

She was busy at her desk scribbling on paper with a pencil. She filled the page, looked at it, then crumbled it into a ball and threw it into the waste basket. I watched her make several.

"What are you doing that you don't like so much?" I asked.

"It's that creepy Dr. Smythe's idea."

"What is?"

"She wants me to make a picture of Daddy."

"How come?"

"How should I know? That's what she gets thirty-five dollars a visit for."

"Gy! Just to talk to her?"

"Well, what do you think, dumbbell? How do you think they make a living?"

I picked up one of her sketches. It was a pretty rotten drawing, if I do say so myself. "That's not Daddy," I said.

Chloris snatched it out of my hands, looked at it, then tore it into a lot of pieces. "How would you know? You don't remember what he looked like."

"Cindy told me."

She goggled. "What? When?"

"At the party for Jeff."

"Okay. What did she tell you?"

I tried to remember. "He was stocky, not too tall, and he was losing his hair."

"You're crazy," Chloris yelled. "He was tall and strong. He had a lot of hair. I remember watching him comb it."

I shrugged. "Okay. Ask Mom."

She rushed to the door and threw it open. Mom had just come in. "Mom, what did Daddy look like?" Chloris yelled.

Mom looked up, frowning. "What?"

Chloris leaned over the railing. "I have to draw a picture. What did Daddy look like?"

"He looked like Gregory Peck. Tall, handsome, dashing."

"C'mom, Mom. I mean it. Really. What did he look like?"

"Well, really he looked like a short stocky man who was losing his hair."

"He wasn't!" Chloris wailed.

"Ask his last wife, Cindy," Mom said. "She helped him lose it."

"You mean he was bald?"

"I didn't say that," Mom said. "I said 'losing his hair.' "

"Well, what's the difference?" Chloris asked.

"Not very much," Mom said.

I pulled Chloris back. "Wait. I've got an idea. Why don't you ask Fidel?"

"Ask him what? He didn't know Daddy."

"I mean Fidel is an artist. All you have to do is tell him what you remember Daddy looked like, and he'll draw it for you."

Her lips parted, her eyes widened happily. "You think he would?"

"Sure," I said. "Fidel is very good-natured. He doesn't care who he does favors for."

"Well, okay," Chloris said. Suddenly she was not sure of herself. "Will you ask him for me?"

"I'll see what I can do."

It was easy as pie. I went down to talk to Fidel about it. He listened without laughing for once. He said to bring Chloris down there and he would draw whatever she said. The studio was still a mess but gradually he was whipping it back in place.

Chloris came in like a shy bride.

Fidel looked at me. "This is supposed to be a private discussion, I think. Perhaps I should be alone with my patron."

I left, feeling only slightly offended. Chloris came out in ten minutes. Her cheeks were flushed and her eyes were shining.

"What happened?" I asked. "Did he take the case?"

Chloris nodded. "He made notes of everything I told him. He's . . . well . . . he really isn't such a creep, after all. I mean, he didn't laugh, or anything."

"Laugh about what?"

Chloris blushed furiously. "I asked him to put on a lot of extra hair."

I was in my room that night. I heard Fidel walking up the steps. He stopped outside Chloris's room and knocked two times. I didn't realize he knew the signal! After he left she called me excitedly, holding her door open and closing it the second I rushed in.

"Isn't it wonderful?" she said.

I looked, following her eyes. Fidel hadn't let Chloris down. He had painted a very big picture, almost ten feet high, almost big enough to cover the wall.

"Is that . . . supposed to be Daddy?" I asked.

"Of course. Don't you like it? Fidel drew it all just as I described Daddy to him. I think it's wonderful." She sank on top of her bed and looked up at the picture lovingly. "Dear Daddy," she said, sighing. "You'll always be near me now."

I swallowed hard and tried to look at the painting again. Fidel had done a wonderful job, all right, used a lot of blue paint and red, the red for the cloak billowing out over Daddy's shoulders, the blue for his costume. The figure looked tall and powerful, his neck wide and strong, his chest massive. His arms were bent, his fists jammed on to his hips. Muscles bulged in his biceps and rippled down the legs spread apart in a poised challenging position. He was standing on top of a mountain, looking prepared to jump off into space any minute.

He wore long gloves and wide-topped boots. His hair was black with luxuriant streaks of blue in it. It was long and full. You could tell he wouldn't be bald for another hundred years.

His eyes looked straight out at us, direct and piercing. His nose was a nice straight nose, not pointed. His teeth were gleaming white, looking powerful enough to bite through a lion. His chin was firm and had a dimple in it. He looked every bit as big and strong as the pictures of Atlas or Hercules, not just strong-looking but super-strong.

"Like it?" Chloris asked again.

I nodded. Poor Chloris. It was exactly the kind of picture she wanted and needed. She would always think somehow our Daddy was really Superman.

CHAPTER 21

THE next few weeks Chloris changed so much I hardly knew it was the same person. She did her homework without bellyaching, kept her room cleaned and her bed made, and not once did she call anybody a creep!

Mom got worried. I could hear her on the phone.

"That child has changed completely, Mother. I don't know what to do. She even smiles at times. At me! And she says good morning. I've even caught her smiling at Fidel."

Grandma said something that made Mom a little uptight.

"How can you say such things? I was always a very pleasant child, as I recall. Perhaps you're confusing me with my brother."

"I don't believe it," Mom said after a pause for listening. "I'm sure you must be exaggerating. Anyhow, I thought you'd be pleased to hear how well Chloris is doing, even though it's made me a nervous wreck wondering what she's up to."

Mom had seen the big picture in Chloris' room

that Fidel had painted, but neither Chloris nor I had bothered telling her it was supposed to be our Daddy.

Fidel had everything back in shape in his studio. He had managed to salvage some things. The big hobby horse, which had only been charred, had been sandpapered and covered with a coat of gleaming blue-black paint. Fidel had carved more of a hollow on the top so there was more room to sit.

"How come?"

Fidel smiled and threw his hands apart. "I think that horse is big enough to hold two little girls."

I didn't care too much for that idea. When I ride I don't need company.

"Your sister," Fidel said, "she is still happy with the big picture?"

"Right on," I said. "How come you made Daddy look like Superman?"

He shrugged and made small waving motions with his hands. "It is like everything in here that I do. A person who buys something from an artist sees only what he wants to see. Some people see it as ugly, some say it is beautiful. With your sister, that picture is only for now. Now is when she needs her Daddy to look so big and strong. One day she will feel strong enough inside herself and no longer need the picture."

That day was coming faster than Fidel or anybody thought.

Mom was on the phone again, holding a letter

that had just come in the morning mail.

"Mother, listen to this. You'll never believe it. Not in a hundred years."

Grandma must have said something flip.

"Oh, all right. Be blasé, if you want. I just received a letter from my attorney. You'll never believe it . . ." Mom waited. "I *am* trying to tell you but you keep interrupting," she said. "You know Cindy has been handling Larry's estate since he died, that the Court appointed her as executor . . . ."

Mom listened patiently, tapping her foot until she got another chance. "Yes, of course," she said on her next turn. "That's why we haven't been getting any money. Cindy's been taking it for her own family. What?"

She listened, then broke in. "I know, Mother. Yes, I probably would do the same thing. Yes, Mother. I know Cindy was his last wife and naturally she would get the bulk of his estate. Why are you so quarrelsome this morning?"

Grandma took her own part for a while.

"All right," Mom said. "Now do you want to hear what my attorney said in his letter, or not? No, I am not being difficult. I think you are."

I really wanted to hear more about the letter but I could tell this was going to take all day so I went outside. Were any deers about? I looked and looked, all over the far ridges, all the way to the top. Then I gave up. Not a sign of one. Nothing. I turned, and nearly jumped out of my shoes.

Not fifty yards away, on the first little ridge

close to our house, where none had ever come before, staring calmly at me was a mama deer with her little baby deer. It was very thin and delicate looking but I had an idea it was willing to make friends. I took a step forward. The mama deer dropped its head and whispered something to the baby. There wasn't any argument. Its eyes went from me to mama. Mama wheeled off and started back up the mountain, the baby tagging closely behind, its mama so sure she had got her message across she didn't bother looking back. In less than a minute they were both gone from sight.

I whistled up at some birds but they had already done all their good morning early calls and were too tired to answer. Either that or, after they had got the whole canyon awake, they had gone back to sleep themselves. Birds can do that to you.

When I went inside the house Mom was still holding the letter and talking about it with Fidel. He was shaking his head, pulling at his lip with his hand. He only does that when he's thinking hard.

"I don't understand it," he said.

"There's no mistake," Mom said. "I called my attorney, Mr. Baker. He assured me he's checked with their lawyer and he's getting the papers sometime today or tomorrow."

Fidel shifted uneasily. "I hope there is no mistake. It could change everything."

"I've told you before that when Larry and I got divorced he agreed to take out insurance policies, enough to see each girl through college."

Fidel raised his hand. "But you also told me he cancelled them before he died."

"Cancelled or let lapse, I'm not sure yet," Mom said. "Cindy's lawyers have been very clever about not letting us see all the papers. Larry ran into debt toward the end and couldn't keep up the payments. He was getting involved in too many things, spreading his money too thin. A few investments went down the drain, so did a lot of his money."

Fidel nodded patiently, and pointed to the letter.

"It says simply that they have finally discovered a new policy in Larry's vault. One they didn't know about. I didn't either, and I'm almost certain Larry had forgotten it completely, too. Otherwise when his money started running out he would have borrowed on it."

"All right. Now you will tell me what it says. Unless this is a series and you want to continue it tonight or tomorrow." Fidel glanced at his watch. "I have a painting to finish . . ."

Mom laughed. "If it's true, you may not have to paint any more for a living. She might want to support you."

Fidel stood up and scratched his hair.

"Oh, I'm just joking," Mom said. "Everybody is so uptight and impatient this morning."

Fidel pointed to the letter and growled something.

"All right," Mom said. "All right. I won't keep you in suspense any longer. The new policy is for fifty thousand dollars. He must have had one for her sister, too, and that was the one he borrowed against until it was all gone."

Fidel sighed. "The little one gets it all?"

Mom nodded. "That's right. He didn't leave Chloris a *dime!*"

CHAPTER 22

It Took a long while for Chloris to get the message that I was an heiress and she wasn't.

"I can't believe it. Daddy wouldn't do a thing like that to me." She walked around her room waving her hands. "I was his favorite little girl. You remember that!"

"I think so," I said. "Something like that."

"You better believe it," Chloris said. "Daddy and I were as close as that." She held up two fingers stuck together.

"I know."

She nodded. "You see. You can remember if you want to. All this time you pretended you didn't."

"I guess so."

"There's one thing that proves it," she said. "Just see if you don't agree."

I sat back. "Like what?"

"He loved me so much and knew I loved him so much that he knew I would give him all the money he wanted. That's why he took it all from me. He knew I trusted him."

"Gy!" I breathed. "I never thought of that."

"You wouldn't. Because you never knew him like I did."

I shook my head and looked sad. "Don't forget I was awful young."

"I know," Chloris said. "That's why he liked me. Because I was more fun to be with. I could talk and everything. You could hardly talk, you were such a baby."

"Gy!"

"Anyway," Chloris said. "That's that."

She walked around her room picking up things and putting them back where they had been. A few more steps and she was standing right under the big glossy picture Fidel had painted of Superman. She shook her head. "You know, there's something wrong with that picture. I don't know exactly what, but somehow it seems wrong to me."

"Like how?" I said cautiously.

"I'm not sure. Fidel did a very good job but I suppose it's difficult trying to do a picture of somebody you've never seen."

"I guess."

She pointed up. "Like I told him Daddy was very strong. Okay. But I don't think he was that strong. Just look at all those muscles. Did you ever see muscles like that on anybody?"

I said I wasn't sure.

She cocked her head. "And there's a little too much hair. Don't you agree?"

I took another look. "You're right, Chloe. A little too much, I think."

She nodded. "The rest of it is sort of okay. I

mean, he really was handsome and tall. But those big boots . . . ." She shook her head. "He never would have worn those kind of boots. Not Daddy."

"How come?"

"They don't look expensive enough. I remember Daddy telling me he always bought the very best things and that was the way for a person to live." She looked up at the painting again. "No," she said. "No way. That picture has got to go. It's a good try but it's not my Daddy."

She took the painting off the wall. Then she got the window open. I heard it crash when it hit the bottom. Chloris made her hands do a quick brushing motion.

"Goodbye, almost-dear Daddy!" She grabbed my arm. "Now let's see what Fidel has to look at in his creepy old studio."

It was okay after that.

All of a sudden Fidel Mancha had two new daughters, one eight and three-quarters, the other eleven going on twelve.

KIN PLATT Kin Platt's admirers are many and the reasons for their admiration are seven memorable books for young people, the latest of which is *Chloris and the Creeps*. The present book falls into the genre of *Hey, Dummy*, the very real and intriguing story of Neil, who is confronted with emotional conflicts dealing not only with his own world but also the world of Alan, a brain-damaged child. The story is on its way to becoming a classic, along with *The Boy Who Could Make Himself Disappear*.

And there are his mystery stories, *Sinbad and Me* and *Mystery of the Witch Who Wouldn't*, which feature Steve; his girlfriend Minerva Landry (the sheriff's daughter); Sinbad, a wonderful English bulldog who doesn't talk but can make himself understood; and a variety of sinister characters. These were preceded by Kin Platt's legendary *Big Max* and *The Blue Man*.

In addition to his writing, Mr. Platt is a well-known cartoonist. His "Mr. and Mrs." and "Duke and Duchess" were known to thousands of readers before he gave up that phase of his career to devote himself exclusively to books.

An ardent golfer and devotee of physical fitness, Kin Platt spends part of each week in the gymnasium and on the golf course. He lives in Los Angeles, although he is equally at home in New York which was his home for most of his early life.